MW00422813

SUZANNAH ROWNTREE

The City Beyond the Glass

SUZANNAH ROWNTREE
travel through time and space

Beware of mirrors...

—suzannah Rowntree

suzannahrowntree.site

First published by Bocfodder Press 2018

Copyright © 2018 by Suzannah Rowntree

All rights reserved. No part of this publication may be reproduced, stored or transmitted in any form or by any means, electronic, mechanical, photocopying, recording, scanning, or otherwise without written permission from the publisher. It is illegal to copy this book, post it to a website, or distribute it by any other means without permission.

This novel is entirely a work of fiction. The names, characters and incidents portrayed in it are the work of the author's imagination. Any resemblance to actual persons, living or dead, events or localities is entirely coincidental.

First edition

Cover art by rebecacovers
Editing by Arielle Bailey

This book was professionally typeset on Reedsy.
Find out more at reedsy.com

Glossary

Doge – the elected head of many Italian city-states during the medieval and Renaissance periods

Carnival – a festival held before the beginning of Lent. Masks are often worn during this period.

Ciel – heavens!

Chopines – A type of women's platform shoe that was popular in the 15th and 16th centuries

Condottiere – mercenary leader

Fondamenta – street parallel to a canal

Loggia – an open, roofed gallery, usually on an upper level

Palazzo – palace

Piano nobile – the principal floor of a large house, containing living quarters

Piano terzo – the third floor of a large house, often containing sleeping quarters

Portego – the central hall of a palazzo

Scuola – a confraternity, or a building in which the confraternity met

Strappado – A form of torture in which the victim is hung from the ceiling by a rope attached to the hands, which are tied together behind the victim's back

Chapter 1.

The mirror on my wall yawned like the entrance to a black cave. A gilt gorgon's-head surmounted the frame, and in the light of my lonely candle, its eyes seemed more baleful than they ever had by daylight.

No time to light more candles to chase away the shadows. I finished pinning a pearl-bordered caul to my hair and took one last glance through the glass.

The girl in the shadowy room wore a simple gown of white silk with small slashed puffs accentuating each shoulder. The candlelight sparked in her kinky copper-coloured hair, but was dim enough to conceal the strain and weariness in the pale face. She looked young. Pretty. Hopeful. Almost as if the last months had never been.

Almost.

I bent to slip on my shoes. First, the flat slippers of silk damask. Fraying again at the toes, and a seam inside had burst. How much did new shoes cost? Could I steal out of the palazzo one of these days and buy some? Or might these be saved with another careful mend?

I picked up my wooden chopines and glanced back into the mirror.

I met the gaze of a masked man. My heart lurched.

He stood behind my shoulder, regarding me silently from the anonymity of a Carnival mask. The mask was white; his cloak was black, and in the darkness it seemed as if his disembodied head floated behind my shoulder, gazing at me with unearthly serenity.

I gave a smothered gasp and turned.

No one stood behind my shoulder. I was alone in the room.

Of course. I swallowed and turned back to the mirror, back to the silent gaze. My voice was high and quavering when I spoke. "Doge?"

"Where are you going tonight, Gemma?" Mild and agreeable, his voice was muffled, as if echoing underwater.

"I have to go out, your serenity. But there's always tomorrow night. We'll all see you tomorrow night."

I sensed his displeasure, but his voice didn't change. "You promised."

"I know, but—"

"Have you grown weary of me, then?"

I shook my head, trying not to let the fear show on my face. "Of course not, Doge! I—"

This time it wasn't the Glass Doge who interrupted me. It was the door bursting open with a sound like doomsday. I wheeled with another racking gasp.

2

"Gemma!" My sister Filippa, at sixteen just a year younger than myself, vibrated with excitement. "It's all clear. Mama's asleep, and the servants have turned in. Come on!"

Fourteen-year-old Lucia, pale as milk and weak as water, was inevitably the one who noticed the dismay on my face. "What's the matter, Gemma?" she quavered.

Filippa's black brows furrowed. "You look like you've seen a ghost."

I couldn't help glancing at the mirror. Only my own eyes met my searching glance. The Glass Doge was gone.

My sisters didn't need to know the Doge had been here. I turned back to them with a shaky smile. "It's nothing. You surprised me, that's all."

That reminded them what I was about to do, and Filippa looked worried. "Are you sure about this, Gemma?"

"You'll be in so much trouble." Lucia clasped her hands.

I shrugged. "Only if I'm caught."

As usual, while Lucia worried, Filippa was practical: "Why risk it? You'll meet the man eventually."

"When it's too late."

"Plenty of girls don't get to see their husbands before the betrothal."

She was right. I didn't have to take this risk. I would see my future husband at the betrothal. But at the thought, a simmer of rage coiled through my stomach. With only daughters to carry on the family line, Papa had long since resigned himself to the extinction of the Caloprini

3

name. Nevertheless, he hoped that the Caloprini trading empire would continue under the watchful guidance of a capable son-in-law. Whoever he'd chosen as my husband, it would be someone like himself. A patrician on the Great Council. Someone respectable. Someone steady. Someone *old*.

I wasn't going to agree to anything until I'd seen the man. No matter what Papa thought. I stood up, snatching mask and gloves from Lucia's hands. "Plenty of girls are gutless."

"Just *think*, Gemma. Even assuming you get admitted to the banquet and find out who it is…what then? What are you going to do? Refuse him?"

"Why not? My consent still matters, doesn't it? Papa wouldn't even tell me his *name*. Why would he behave like that unless he knew I'd object?" I yanked on my gloves and tied the black Carnival mask over my face. "I'm sick of it, Filippa. All my life I've been locked behind bars. Tonight, *I* take control."

"That's what you said the night we met the Doge."

"Did I?" Filippa had an unsettling habit of remembering things like that. "Well, this time it's true."

"What *about* the Glass Doge?" Lucia wondered as she and Filippa trailed me to the door.

"What about him?" I snapped with a bravado I didn't feel.

"You always say we've promised…"

I turned back on her. "The Doge beyond the glass is

4

the least of our worries right now. Once I'm married, you get sent back to the convent, remember?"

Her forehead wrinkled in distress. "I know."

It was cruel to remind her of it. I knew neither Lucia nor Filippa wanted to spend the rest of their lives locked inside Saint Mary of the Virgins, never again to set foot beyond its walls. As little as I wanted to marry a stranger, I had to be grateful I was not destined for the same fate.

But it would be crueller still to let her know the Doge's true nature."Don't worry. The Doge has excused us for tonight." If it wasn't strictly the truth he'd have to blame me, not them. "Take the opportunity for a full night's sleep. We'll see him again tomorrow."

I cracked the door open. Beyond, the portego of our palazzo was lit only by a glimmer of light through the colonnaded windows of the loggia above the Grand Canal. As the girls had promised, there was no light showing under the door of the room to the loggia's right. Mama, as usual, had drugged herself into a fretful sleep. The three of us tiptoed across the hall and stole downstairs.

Below, the piano nobile was very similar, a hall fronting the canal with large rooms to either side. Below that again was the ground floor, which, apart from the large and ornate entrance hall, was devoted to storage, servants, and sculleries.

The hall was still dimly lit for Papa's return. The servants had taken the opportunity to slacken off: early as it was, most of the lights were out in their rooms. Strange

5

how empty and exhausted the house always seemed with him gone, like the husks left in a spider's web. The three of us tiptoed soundlessly across the floor of the portego and emerged into the one small corner of our land that was devoted to a courtyard and as many plants as we could coax to grow here.

Filippa dipped into her bodice to produce a wrought-iron key. I sat down on a bench to pull on my chopines. At just four inches, the velvet-covered wooden platforms added little to my already gangly height. But Papa thought women looked silly stalking around like jesters with a servant at each hand to prop them up, and for once, I agreed with him.

As I took my first cautious step in the dark, my shoe wobbled dangerously on the edge of a bit of pavement. Lucia caught me with a squeal.

"Shh!" Filippa and I hissed at the same moment. For a few heartbeats we stood motionless, listening for some sign that Lucia's voice had carried to the servants. But of course, even if they heard, why should they care?

I nodded to Filippa.

She crossed the courtyard in a few steps and stabbed the key at the lock several times before it slid home and the lock creaked open. I clacked across the pavement and caught her shoulder before she could swing the gate open. Filippa looked up at me, her face nothing but a pale blur in the darkness of night.

"Be careful, Gemma."

I knew then that she was just as worried as Lucia. Maybe I ought to have been frightened too. But I wasn't; I was much too excited. Taking the key from her, I closed my hand around the gate and yanked it open so suddenly the hinges forgot to squeak. The damp alleyway beyond waited blackly before us.

I'd given them my instructions upstairs; they wouldn't wait up for me. I slipped through and closed the gate as quickly as I had opened it. The key I nestled under my stays. My last sight was of Lucia wringing her hands with helpless fluttering motions.

I wanted to laugh at her. I thought my heart was going to soar out of my chest. For the first time in my life, I had escaped my prison.

The palazzo lay behind me, its watchful spirits no longer able to examine my every move.

Venice awaited.

* * *

You may smile, but I wasn't exaggerating when I said I'd lived my whole life behind bars. It was the literal truth. I was just seven and my sisters were even younger when we were sent to be educated at the most prestigious convent in Venice. From the beginning we knew that two of us would spend the rest of our lives there. We might do it willingly, out of love for God, like some of the sisters did. Or we might do it with tears and sighs and small acts of

7

rebellion like hundreds of others, but it would happen whether we wanted it or not.

Oh yes, there were bars at Saint Mary of the Virgin. Bars, and locks, and thick walls that blocked the sun.

Even so, some of us escaped: those few destined for marriage. For years, I'd longed for the day when the gates would open. Six months ago, they had. I was so eager to leave that I'd barely slept for a whole week, worrying that something might go wrong. That I might never escape into the sunlight and the fresh air and the freedom of Venice.

Something did go wrong. Papa brought us home, only to shut us up behind a new set of walls while he set to work arranging my marriage. The palazzo wasn't the home I'd remembered. My parents were strangers, even to each other. And at least the convent had given us work to do. Here, we could only look out the windows, staring at passers-by we would never speak to travelling to places we would never see.

Even the Glass Doge was preferable to boredom.

Now, Papa meant to lock me into a marriage with someone I'd never met. But I wouldn't take it quietly, I vowed. I would have my say in this if it was the last thing I ever did.

In the alley beyond our gate, it was so dark I could barely see my own hand in front of my face. This was unexpected, but I put my gloved fingertips against our garden wall and began to walk.

I went south toward the Grand Canal. I had a few coins in my purse, enough to hire a gondola. Papa was at a banquet with his confraternity just a short distance away—I didn't remember exactly how to find the Scuola Grande di San Marco, but the gondolier would. As I clacked through the alley with mounting excitement, I wished it was further. I wanted to see as much of the city as I could.

The dark alley opened and released me into a narrow courtyard that terminated in a brief wooden jetty. It was a little lighter here, but the looming back walls on each side blocked out most of the light. A little lamplight filtered through windows. February breathed crisp and damp down my neck. On the jetty, a fog-haloed lantern bobbed as another woman, dressed in a glinting skirt, stepped precariously into a gondola. The cavalier helping her stepped in after them and, with a swish of oars, the gondola took them away.

The lantern turned and came back toward me. A link-boy, barely as high as my elbow, pungent as the dungheap in which he probably slept. "Fetch you a gondola, signorina?"

I gave him a silver coin and followed him to the jetty. I was not frightened. I knew fear; it breathed out of the walls of my house, it lurked in the mirrors. This was freedom.

I ought to have done this long ago.

I didn't have to wait long for a gondola. Ghostly

lanterns glided to and fro on the black waters. Occasional snatches of talk or laughter echoed across the water. I stepped down into the first gondola that paused to collect me from the jetty and seated myself well forward in the black boat, leaning from the small cabin to absorb every sight. Even under the thick pall of night, Venice was far more alive than I had ever imagined. Eddying currents of air brought me everything from the stench of decay to the floral whiff of perfume. Men and women floated by me, anonymous in masks, the lamplight sparking flame-colours from their clothing.

I *ought* to have done this long ago. I gripped the gunwale as a lighted tavern drifted by. Through its misted windows, there filtered a skirling music, exotic and wild. We'd turned into a narrower canal, and I could have made one step of it from the gondola to the doorstep. I could have plunged into the lights and sounds and smells of this wonderful city and lost myself.

At the convent, they whispered about girls who sneaked out to meet lovers in the streets, who went dancing in taverns with cutpurses and gypsies. Folly, I'd always thought it. I was a good girl. I had principles.

Tonight, for the first time, I understood what drew them out into the night. If this was the real Venice, it was better than any enchantment.

Once I reached the scuola I would be back among Papa's kind of people: staid citizens with paunches and purses to guard, their conversation droning on about how many bales of wool they'd lost to the Turks this year, or how much further the price of pepper had dropped now that the Portuguese were bringing it home direct from India, or how much the market for octavo books had grown in the last quarter.

Pepper and books, when life was passing them by!

Still, I had a job to do, and it would be exciting to speak to Papa's friends from behind a mask, pretending to be someone I wasn't. Just as we approached an arching footbridge, the gondola slid to a halt. I leaned forward and recognised the massive brick façade of the great basilica of Saint John and Saint Paul on the other side of the campo. On the right, the equestrian statue of the condottiere Colleoni was little more than a glinting bronze outline. The white building to the left of the basilica, torches outlining its classical arches and light glowing in the windows, was the scuola. I'd been here once before, at a previous banquet.

I paid the gondolier and was two steps into the empty campo before doubt hit me. What if Papa recognised me—by my clothes, my walk, my hair? I touched my lips with my tongue, then gave myself a mental shake. I was already so close. Was I going to lose my nerve *now?*

"I am Piera Cardoni," I rehearsed under my breath. "I've got a message for Marco Tiepolo." I had no idea if that would get me through the door, but I thought I had a chance, especially if I used the name of Marco's old nurse. I'd wheedle him into bringing me into the banquet, where

I could spy on Papa and his guest. If Marco was still the daredevil I remembered from childhood, he'd tease me without mercy, but he'd do what I asked.

I knew better than to hope that someone like Marco would be Papa's choice. But I could stop for a moment and wish.

My gondola had faded into the night. I squared my shoulders and stepped toward the scuola.

This time, it wasn't doubt that halted me, it was a sudden burst of running footsteps on the footbridge behind me. I turned.

The man's cloak flapped like the wings of a gigantic bird of prey as he bore down on me. "Giovanna!" he called, reaching out.

I backed. There was nobody else here. Nobody but me. The torchlight reflected off the stranger's white mask as he stopped in front of me. Before his cloak stopped moving, he'd doffed his bonnet, seized my hand and brushed it with the cold porcelain lips of his mask.

"You're mistaken, signor." I tried to pull my hand away, but his grip closed like a vice on my fingers and my words ended on a gasp of pain.

"Maybe, but for heaven's sake don't make a fuss and you'll be well paid, signorina. Walk a little way with me."

He folded my arm into the crook of his elbow and swept me along with him. Not toward the scuola.

Toward the street leading into darkness beyond Colleoni.

12

"No!" I protested. Then my chopine turned beneath my foot, and I almost fell.

"Shh!" He didn't slacken, forcing me to abandon the overshoes and bundle up my overlong skirts to keep them off the ground. Nervous tremors jittered up through his body and into my arm. Whoever this man was, he was every bit as frightened as me.

I dropped my voice to a panicked whisper. "Let go of me! What are you doing? What do you want?"

"A bodyguard." Past the statue. Out of the light. Into the darkness of a narrow alley.

From behind I heard hurrying feet, felt the man's body react as he too registered the presence of others.

"A *bodyguard?*"

"Don't look back." He never let up his pace. He had me pulled against his left side, the guard of his rapier jammed into my ribs. Even so, there was barely space in the narrow way for both of us side-by-side. Now he reached across his body with his free right and loosened the blade in the sheath. "The men hunting me don't want witnesses. Pray they won't come looking for trouble."

His accent made it clear he was a foreigner. Someone from the mainland. Doubly a stranger, and less to be trusted.

My head whirled. How did this happen? One moment I was standing on a campo in my beautiful Venice, drunk on freedom with the end of my journey in sight. The next I was being dragged through a dark street by someone who was about to get me killed.

The footsteps behind us edged closer.

"Speak," the stranger said. "Let them hear your voice."

I said the first thing that came into my head. "My father is on the Great Council, and if I come to any harm, they will have you sent to the galleys."

"Plague!" For a moment he stopped and stared at me. Much good it did him in the dark. "The Great Council?" He touched the fabric of my cloak. "You're no common harlot. San Osanna! You're one of the expensive ones, aren't you? You were alone—I thought—Plague!"

The footsteps behind us picked up speed. The stranger burst into motion again. My face was hot behind the mask as I stumbled to keep up. He thought I was a prostitute? I would have vented my indignation if it hadn't been clear to both of us that the stranger's gambit had failed. Whoever was following us meant to force a confrontation.

"Run," he said.

The alley's mouth was a slit of not-so-dark in front of us. Then light like a small sun broke around the corner. I saw the newcomer in parts, not whole: fire and steel. Mask and torch. Cloak and sword.

He saw us and his swordpoint flicked up. He lifted his torch. Light poured down on us.

The stranger swore under his breath, coming to a halt and turning, sweeping me against the wall with one hand. Winks of light scattered from the ring on his littlest finger, a big silver gorgon's-head with its mouth open in a silent howl. Just like the head that topped my mirror.

A common good luck charm. But it reminded me of the Glass Doge, who hadn't wanted me to leave him tonight. The bottom dropped out of my stomach. Even in the city, was I being watched?

Footsteps scuffled in the dark. Two masked men blocked the alley that led to the campo and my father, torchlight flickering down the lethal shapes of dagger and rapier. The stranger brushed past me and drew his sword. "Try not to get in the way, signorina."

On my left, the man with the torch stood motionless. On my right, the first of our two assailants inched closer, his blades moving restlessly, seeking the moment to strike. Head down, shoulders and hips slinking, he reminded me of nothing so much as a great, hungry cat.

I wished I could do something. But they didn't prepare you for this at the convent.

The stranger caught his breath and exploded into motion. His lunge took him to full extension, forcing the other to retreat. Then he was up and moving forward, the sound of swords horribly loud between the suffocating walls of the alley.

At the opening of the alley, the torchbearer took a step toward me.

"Help!" I shrieked, but no sound of rescue came from the streets beyond. I gulped as the torchbearer stepped forward again. From what the stranger said, these men

15

wouldn't think twice of killing me to silence me. But if he turned to help me, his attackers would stab him in the back.

My life depended on me. I didn't have a weapon, but I was wearing pearls. In one quick movement, I unlatched the string from my neck and offered it to the torchbearer. "Let me pass, signor. I've got nothing to do with this, and I won't say a word."

The torchbearer took another step toward me, and this time I let him come. The swordpoint lowered, then shot into the sheath, and I let out a gasp of relief. "Thank you."

He reached for the pearls. But instead of taking them, he wrapped his fingers around my wrist and yanked forward. The torchlight blinked as he moved. I screamed again.

He smelled of sweat and onions and he was much better at this than I was, even with only one hand free. He knocked me against the wall, and before the stars cleared from my eyes, he had his left hand around my neck in a grip that only got tighter as I struggled. "Stand still," he hissed, and then raised his voice. "Eh, Gonzaga!"

No answer.

A few paces up the alley, the stranger who'd gotten me into this mess made another lunge. Steel flashed. Someone yelled, a peculiarly chilling and throaty cry. The hand on my neck tightened. "*Gonzaga!* Drop your sword!"

The stranger retreated, put his back to the wall, and risked a glance in our direction. But no more than a glance. He didn't obey my captor's command; he kept his guard up.

One of his enemies was slumped against the wall, his breath laboured and whistling. The other leaned over his fallen comrade. There was a moment of silence.

"I told Sforza I'd pay." The stranger—Gonzaga—seemed a little breathless. Otherwise, he spoke casually, as if taking up the thread of an ongoing conversation. "All I need is time."

"Fool, you can't pay for this! Who did you think you were dealing with, a peppercorn-merchant? Sforza wants the full price of the contract returned to him. He wants to see the colour of your money or the colour of your guts by Lent, and he's not choosy about which."

Sforza? As in the ruling house of Milan? Whoever Gonzaga was, he'd offended some very important people.

"I don't have the money," Gonzaga said patiently. "But I will."

The whistling breaths of the wounded man faded away. The other ruffian sank into a fighter's crouch, ready to resume the fight.

"Are you sure about this?" Gonzaga spoke as casually as before, but his body tensed infinitesimally. "If I kill you, it makes no difference to Sforza. He'll just send someone else. On the other hand, we could cut a deal. You walk away, I'll find a ship out of Venice, and you can tell the duke I left town."

I wondered how I fitted into this deal.

The hand at my throat tightened, making the blood thunder in my head. "No deals! Drop your blades, or the wench dies!"

I couldn't speak. Couldn't see.

But I could hear.

"Kill her then." Gonzaga gave a soft snort of amusement. "Do I seem to care?"

He didn't mean it. He was bluffing.

"I'll do it!"

The hand tightened inexorably on my throat, cutting off the pulse. My head was going to explode. I grabbed feebly at the wrist.

Dimly, the clash of swords came to my ears. Holy saints, he did mean it. He wasn't even paying attention. He was going to discard me as nonchalantly as he'd forced me into accompanying him.

I don't know why, in that moment, I thought of Lucia. Lucia sniffling:

"I told her it was dangerous."

Plague her!

I let go of the hand at my neck and reached out with clawed fingers. It had to be pure luck, or my guardian angel, that my fingers found the eyeholes of his mask. I hooked and tore, and the hand left my throat with a roar of anger. Then it swung back and smashed into my cheekbone.

Mask awry, I tumbled blindly to the damp stones of the alleyway. No time to right the mask: I tore it from

18

my face. My overlong skirts hampered me as I struggled to rise. The man with the torch fumbled for his rapier.

Then just as I staggered to my feet, the sweetest sound in the world: "Down swords! Down swords! In the name of the Republic!"

The Night Watch. Thank heaven.

They flocked over the footbridge at a run and poured into the alleyway with their torches held high. My captor of a moment ago dropped his own torch on the ground with a volley of curses.

"Stand, on your peril," boomed the same stentorian voice.

Neither Gonzaga nor his assailant took the slightest notice. Instead, by some silent agreement they lowered their swords and bolted. Seeing my way open, I followed them, hopping over the dead man and racing for the other end of the alley and the open campo.

Shouts and pounding feet from behind. Maybe it was the third man, the one who'd nearly choked me. Maybe it was the Watch. I didn't want either of them to catch me. With a fresh burst of speed, I made it into the campo.

Lights. Voices. Evidently the fight in the alley had gone on too long, had attracted the attention of more than just the Night Watch. The scuola had emptied and the merchants and patricians milled chattering and gawking on the pavement outside, trailed by their torchbearers. I skidded to a stop and clapped a hand to my naked face.

My mask. My *mask!*

Someone breathed heavily in my ear, and a gentle but firm hand fastened on my elbow. "Signorina, please don't try to run. We'll be requiring your testimony."

Gonzaga and the other attacker had vanished. The knot of citizens in front of the scuola flocked curiously toward us. It was futile to try to hide, but I whipped around, pulling at the Watchman's grip. "Please! I lost my mask. I can't be seen. Won't you…"

Then I saw the splendid fur trim on his neck and wrists. His unmasked face, recognisable in the flickering torchlight. This was not just any Watchman: it was one of their commanders, a Lord of the Night.

He blinked. "Gemma *Caloprini?*"

"Signor Tiepolo," I stammered. Marco's father was a Lord of the Night? "This is all a terrible mistake. Please don't let my father see me."

He stared at me blankly for a moment and then flushed as red as if I'd slapped him. Instantly, he started toward the scuola, towing me behind him. "Caloprini!" he boomed.

"Tiepolo? What is it?" My father's voice. I squawked in protest as Tiepolo pushed me forward. I heard rather than saw Papa's reaction, the sharp hiss of indrawn breath, the mutter of "Plague!"

"Yes," Tiepolo bit, "very unfortunate."

"Signorina?" Someone was standing next to Papa. I looked up into the shocked eyes of Marco himself.

"I'm sure there's some explanation for this." Papa was

beginning to recover, but I still didn't understand.

Not until Tiepolo shook his head. "No. The betrothal is off."

* * *

Papa stepped forward to shield me from the stares of his scuola brothers. A useless gesture, and one I knew by now to be empty. It was his own reputation Papa worried about, not mine.

"Should men of our standing do their business in the common streets, Nicolo? We owe each other a better hearing, I think."

He and Tiepolo arranged it between them just as they had arranged our marriage: in hurried undertones, while Marco and I stared at each other in the same mute shock. The end of it was that Marco's father sent him home and Papa hurried me into the next gondola, seating me far back in the cabin with no chance to see or be seen.

No one said a word as we rode home. As for me, I doubt I could have spoken if I'd tried. As my fighting reflexes drained away, I began to shake uncontrollably.

Marco Tiepolo was the man my father had picked for me.

Laughing, devil-may-care Marco. Handsome, reckless Marco, whom I'd adored from afar since we were both children.

My father had picked Marco for me despite all my

fears. And now, of course, it would come to nothing. Girls caught wandering Venice at night in the company of strangers did not marry.

I wished they would talk. Even about peppercorns.

When we finally reached the palazzo, a yawning servant opened the door. The distinctive lemon-and-cloves smell of my house, my prison, reached out to me. My one night of freedom was done.

Papa led the way up to the piano nobile where he had his study. Tiepolo came last, like a guard bringing up the rear. A door led directly off the portego into the study, but as I moved to enter, Papa waved me back.

"Go and clean yourself up, Gemma. I'll send for you when I want you."

I don't know what made me think he'd actually want to speak to me, to understand my actions. But this dismissal was one step too far. "I don't need to clean myself up, I need to tell you what happened!"

From the staircase came whispers and rustling. Filippa and Lucia must be eavesdropping.

Papa's face tightened, but he didn't raise his voice. "Signor Tiepolo will tell me."

"He doesn't know any more about it than you do! I was there by *mistake*, Papa."

He hesitated and glanced sideways at Tiepolo. "Fine. Tell me."

I swallowed tightly. "You never told me it was going to be Marco, and I had to know. I was trying to get into the scuola and find out who it would be."

"And the brawl?"

"I don't know what that was about. Just as I reached the campo, a foreigner came and dragged me into the alley. He said the duke's men wouldn't try to kill him if he wasn't alone. He was wrong." I regained confidence now that Papa was listening. He and I both wanted to give a good explanation for what had happened tonight.

"Which duke?" Tiepolo seemed curious.

"Sforza."

Papa gave a tight nod. "Will you swear that you never saw any of those men before tonight, Gemma?"

My cheeks heated. "Do you really think I would be so shameless?"

"Keep your voice down! I should hope not." But he was pleased with my answer. He swung toward Tiepolo. "I assume your men apprehended the brawlers. I'd be obliged if they were put to the question on this."

"We have one of them. Rest assured he'll be questioned."

"Good. Gemma, you can go. Nicolo, come into the study. I'm sure we can come to an agreement…"

"One moment." To my astonishment, Tiepolo pointed at my feet. "May I see the signorina's shoe, please?"

I still had my too-long skirts bunched up in my arms, and since Tiepolo had mounted the stairs behind me, he would have had a clear view of my feet. Heart sinking, I dropped the skirt to hide them. "My shoe?"

He turned to Papa. "I'm a Lord of the Night. It's my

23

business to observe details. The shoe, please."

Papa nodded to me. There was no helping it. Reluctantly, I kicked off my slipper and stepped back, leaving it for Tiepolo to retrieve.

Just a trumpery thing of glass beads and silk. A dancing-slipper meant to be worn out and thrown away.

Well overdue to be thrown away.

Tiepolo lifted it to the light and turned it over and over for a long time in silence. Then for the first time, he spoke to me directly. "Your shoes tell a different story, signorina."

Papa snatched the shoe from him. Inspected the frayed fabric, the stains, the soles that had worn thin.

"Are you sure you told us the truth?" A grim smile twitched the corner of Tiepolo's mouth. "Are you sure you never ventured into the city alone?"

From the stairs came a moth-flutter of movement. Footsteps crept across the ceiling. My sisters had retreated from the stairwell. Overcome by doubt? Anxious not to be implicated in my downfall?

Unexpectedly, it was Papa who saved me. "That's nonsense, signor. My daughter has worn these shoes everywhere for a whole year. Of course they are worn out."

I saw the flicker of calculation in his eyes. He knew as well as I did that the shoes weren't more than three months old and had barely been worn twice, to his knowledge. But he'd say anything to save face. As he returned my shoe, he shot me a look that warned me to be silent. I didn't need to be told. Maybe Tiepolo wouldn't let his son marry me, but I was fighting now for my right to be married at all. If I lost my character, I was doomed to imprisonment at the convent. So I tilted my chin and held my peace.

More footsteps above. Were they even *trying* to be discreet?

"If you say so, Caloprini." Tiepolo seemed dubious. "Still, regarding my son, there can be no question of a match now. The signorina was seen in the open street. Marco was eager for this marriage, but now, of course, I will be withdrawing my permission. Marco won't complain. I've raised him to be conscious of his honour."

Would Marco really turn up his nose at me because of this? When everyone *knew* how he amused himself. It wasn't fair. And I was opening my mouth to say so when something far worse happened.

"Lucia, *no*," Filippa hissed from somewhere on the staircase. *"Lucia!"*

My youngest sister jounced down the final steps and into view. Her face was pale and determined, her eyes huge as cartwheels.

Her arms, full of ruined shoes.

She took five steps toward us and thrust her own slippers and Filippa's under Papa's nose. "See, Papa? Ours are worn out too, and we've had them even less time than Gemma. If you blame her for leaving the house at night,

25

you have to blame all of us."

There was a long and awkward silence.

Papa and Tiepolo looked at each other. Cold conscious-
ness of triumph lit the Night Lord's eyes. "I really think
there can be no point in discussing this further, Gennaro."

"I agree." Papa held himself stiffly upright, but the air
seemed heavy with thunder. "You had better go. I have a
house to put in order."

* * *

We had both shouted, and now Lucia was crying.

"I thought that when he saw all our shoes, he'd know
Gemma was a good girl like us!"

"Don't be a fool!" Filippa snapped at her. She'd come
downstairs, and now the three of us were crowded into
the study while Papa showed Signor Tiepolo to the door.
"You didn't prove that Gemma was a good girl! You
dishonoured us all!"

"I didn't realise!"

Filippa stamped her foot. "I would have *told* you if you'd
listened!"

I let my hands fall from my temples. "Will you stop it,
both of you? I nearly got *killed* tonight." I was shaking
again. "I nearly got killed, and all anyone cares about is
my reputation!"

That got their attention. "Ohhh, Gemma," Lucia
hiccupped with useless and waterlogged sympathy.

"What happened?" Filippa knitted her dark brows. "Was it the Glass Doge?"

I gave a brittle laugh. "The Glass Doge, what on earth? No…"

Then I remembered the gorgon ring on Gonzaga's hand, and my fears that somehow the Doge had brought me bad luck.

"No." I pushed the fears to the back of my mind. "Just a bravo from the mainland."

In the silence that followed, Papa's footsteps sounded on the stair. Filippa turned on me, gripping my arm. "Gemma! What are we going to say?"

There was no time to think, to feel. "Nothing," I breathed. "Let me do the talking."

Papa came in and shut the door with an precise *snick*. In silence, he sat down and stared at us over the ragged line of shoes on his desk. When he spoke, an icy calm was clamped down hard over his anger.

"You ought to have taken a servant, Gemma. *San Marco,* there was no need to leave the palazzo! If I'd known what it meant to you, I would have told you his name!"

"You knew full well what it meant to me," I sparked back at him. "I *asked!*"

"Do not flout me, Gemma!" His shout made me flinch. "Do you have any idea what dishonour you have brought on this family? A thousand years, Gemma! A thousand years of Caloprinis in Venice! I have no son, and if I cannot marry my daughter well, that legacy ends. The

27

end of one of the oldest families in Venice."

"What do we have besides age?" I said dully.

"We have blood! We have a name! We have a hand on the helm of Venice herself! And the three of you have squandered it in a single night. No one will marry any of you now." He threw out a despairing hand. "You might as well go back to Saint Mary in the morning. And then I had better drink nightshade."

Saint Mary. Cold rage crawled down my neck. The convent. Again. It was the one hope I'd clung to that no matter what happened, no matter who I married, no matter what the Glass Doge might ask, at least I would never again be shut behind the walls of Saint Mary of the Virgins.

Papa spoke again. "First, an explanation. I bought these shoes new not three months ago. Where have you been? Who were you meeting?"

My sisters didn't answer. Just looked at me. I didn't say a word. There was no mirror in Papa's study, just two small windows with jewel-tinted glass. At night there was no colour visible, just the reflected candlelight clear and sharp like a terrestrial star. Like the eye of God.

Like the eye of someone who might as well be.

I stared at the dark glass above Papa's head and spoke as evenly as I could. "I met him half a year ago when you took us out of the convent. I don't know if he's Venetian or not. I still don't know his name. But he promised freedom. Music. Dancing. I'd been locked up for ten

28

years, so I went with him. Of *course* I went with him."

With a tiny metallic *snap*, a penknife broke between my father's white-knuckled hands.

"He kept his promise, Papa." I smiled tightly. "It was all he said and more."

My sisters stared at me, openmouthed. They knew I was telling the strict truth, but that I would say it like this struck them with horror.

Good. I couldn't risk them saying anything. Maybe I'd already said too much. Didn't I know that the Glass Doge was a secret I must guard with my life?

Papa's face was ashen, a trickle of blood oozing unheeded from his finger where the knife had caught it. "And your sisters? You took Filippa and Lucia with you?"

"May prisoners not dream of escaping?"

"You corrupted them."

"Think so if you wish." I spat the words with contempt. "Heaven knows we are all innocent. But that doesn't count for anything with you, does it? We could be *saints* and you'd still lock us away. I could have died tonight, or worse. But you don't care about me. All you care about is preserving our reputation long enough to make a rich match."

"That's enough." White to the lips, Papa didn't bother to raise his voice. "Tell me where to find this man. He'll have to marry one of you."

I had no breath.

Marry the Doge beyond the glass?

29

The one bright eye of candlelight glared at me from the dark glass. I swallowed once before I spoke.

"Believe me, Papa. He's not for the like of us to meddle with."

He slammed his open palm against the desk. "Ciel, Gemma! Do you persist in flouting me?"

I didn't bother answering. Silent mutiny was always best at the convent, and it had proven effective with Papa too.

When he had shouted at us for a while with no effect, he stood and glared at us.

"Go to bed, all of you. We'll discuss this again in the morning."

* * *

Anger and useless worry kept me awake until dawn, and I woke the next morning with sticky eyes and a pounding head. I would have turned over and tried to sleep again but for the indistinct voices coming from Mama's room next door.

The mirror reflected early sunlight into my right eye. From the gorgon's-head atop the frame, blank gold eyes stared at me, and the mouth howled silently as if frozen in a moment of endless horror. As if it was trapped and would never be free.

I shuddered and sat up. Lucia sat next to the window embroidering gloves, a listless droop in the corner of her

30

mouth. But Filippa, ever practical, had her ear pressed to the wall that divided us from Mama's room.

"It's *Papa*," she whispered when she saw my questioning look.

Our parents lived in the same house, but they behaved like strangers. Sometime in the last ten years, Mama had become an invalid. Constantly sleeping, never quite in her full wits because of the drugs she took, she emerged from her room only for periodic bursts of life which soon burned out, leaving her once again limp in her bed. By now, she seemed not so much a member of the household as just one more of the ghosts that haunted it.

I didn't know why Papa was talking to her, but it couldn't be a good sign.

The voices ceased, a door creaked, and Filippa left the wall with a worried scowl.

I reached for my comb and set to work on my hair. "What did they say?"

Filippa hitched a shoulder. "He said she was a bad mother for not watching us better. She asked if he was looking for a reason to divorce her."

A divorce? That would give Papa the chance to remarry, to father the son he'd always wanted. But it would also mean repaying Mama's dowry and losing the lucrative investments her brothers made in his shipments of glass and slaves.

"What did he say to that?"

"Nothing." Filippa clearly didn't want to talk about it.

31

Instead, she sat on the end of the bed, her mouth screwed shut as if she was about to cry, her thick black brows a bar shadowing her eyes. I could not think of anything comforting to say. I got up and pulled a loose gown over my shift.

"Did Mama say anything else?"

She shook her head.

Why did my heart fall at the news? Mama would never save us; I ought to have known that. I turned my mind to the larger question.

"Papa won't send me to the nunnery. He wants a son-in-law for the business. He'll probably try to marry me off to anyone who will take me." I squared my shoulders and turned to the mirror to finish doing my hair.

This morning, in the sunlight, there was only my own reflection to face me.

"Aren't you going to tell him about the Glass Doge?" Lucia's voice was hushed and apologetic, still mindful of her mistake last night.

"What good would that do?"

"He thinks you were going out into the city. Why did you say it like that, Gemma? You made it all sound so *wrong*."

"I only said what he was already thinking. What reason have we given him to suppose such things?" I yanked angrily at my tangled hair. "Anyway, he won't be any happier if we tell him where we've really been. Even if he believes us."

"Maybe he *would* believe us." Filippa spoke in a hushed voice. "And that would be much, much worse."

It would be. But I'd never told *her* that. A prickle walked my neck. How much did she know?

Lucia's eyes were like big silver groats. "Why? Why would that be worse?"

Filippa stared at her. "Don't you realise what the Glass Doge really is?"

I let out a muted screech.

"Gemma?"

"It's nothing." I put a finger in my mouth. "Stabbed myself with a pin."

I knew what Filippa was hinting at. The Glass Doge was no natural being. If anyone found out about him, we wouldn't be sent to a convent, we'd be sent to the Inquisitors.

How did she know? I'd kept my fears a secret from both my sisters, afraid that if I ever told them about the Doge's true nature, he'd overhear us. Maybe he'd wonder if we were about to become a threat to him. And I didn't want to imagine what might happen then.

My neck was still prickling. Filippa was always more perceptive than Lucia. I should be more careful.

Thankfully, Maria entered with our breakfast and put an end to the conversation. A Tartar woman with slanted eyes and a pale complexion, Maria had come all the way from the Black Sea as a girl on one of Papa's slave vessels, and he'd selected her as a wedding present for Mama. All these years later, Maria was the one who bore the burden of Mama's illness: cleaning her room, preparing her doses, catering to her whims as few freedwomen would have. Mama talked about emancipating her, but we all knew it wouldn't happen. Maria was too useful, and knew too much about our family, to be allowed her freedom.

But she wasn't the one who usually waited on us in the morning. Since leaving the convent, we had a maid of our own. Was she sick this morning? Or was Papa entrusting one more dangerous family secret to Maria's flat bosom?

"Signorina Gemma?" She'd never lost the peculiar accent of her birth. "The signor asks you to wait on him in the study as soon as you've eaten."

Dressed for the day, I strode to the door, brushing aside Lucia's offer of food. "I'm not hungry." I'd been dreading this confrontation with Papa, but now the moment had come I just wanted to get it over with.

I entered the study with my courage screwed up for battle, but something about Papa this morning stopped me in my furious tracks. He sat with clasped hands staring at the six shoes on his desk. When he looked up at me, I saw every single line in his face, the skin sagging and colourless.

His first words surprised me even more. "We spoke in anger last night, Gemma. Forgive me."

I wasn't ready for that. Tears crawled up my throat. "You accused me of corrupting my sisters. Do you trust me so little?"

He stared at his desk. "I don't know, Gemma. I thought I did. But these…" A nod at the shoes. "And now, the gossip… Word that you go roaming the streets at night. Word that—well, never mind. You can imagine. All three of you. It will be a miracle if I am able to find a husband for any of you now."

My tears dried on cheeks like embers. How like Papa only to care what other people thought.

He looked at me pleadingly. "As your father, I have the right to know where you go and what you do there."

I shouldn't even have hinted at the Glass Doge's existence last night. I couldn't risk saying anything else. I folded my arms. "Ask the servants. They'll tell you we don't leave our room."

"I'm not asking the servants. I'm asking you."

"Would you believe me if I told you?"

He looked at me, and then at the shoes. "That would depend on what you said."

I could say nothing.

Papa leaned back in his chair, defeated. "There are still those who would welcome an alliance with the House of Caloprini. Poorer patricians. Cadet branches. I might offer Lucia, maybe. She looks…innocent."

"*Looks?* She *is* innocent!" My hands folded into fists. "An innocent fool. Surely that ought to be obvious, after last night."

"Which is why she may yet save us." Papa rubbed a hand across his forehead. "Lucia will do."

"And Filippa and me?"

"It will have to be the convent. No," he added as I opened my mouth to protest. "You knew what you were doing. You knew most families can only afford a good match for one son and one daughter in each generation. You had your chance."

And lost it. No one knew that more keenly than me. "Don't forget that you had a hand in this, Papa. If I'd known it was Marco, I'd never have left the house."

"I'll do it differently this time."

Something in his shuttered look woke my suspicions. "She'll get to meet him?"

"Yes." His discomfort intensified. I narrowed my eyes.

"What are you going to do, Papa?"

"Business." He straightened, fidgeting with a quill pen. "Tiepolo has not guarded his tongue. All Venice knows what happened here last night. The occasion calls for boldness. I will make it known that I will bestow Lucia and a *sizeable* dowry on the suitor who discovers where you go and why your shoes are worn out. He will watch you, day and night, until the mystery is solved."

"Day *and* night?" He couldn't be serious.

He gave me a look that promised he was deadly serious.

"This is outrageous! If you want someone to watch us, why not do it yourself?"

"Because if I say my daughters are honest, who will believe me? No. This is a way to seize control of the gossip. To rebuild the Caloprini name."

36

I was speechless for a moment. Somehow, I had still underestimated Papa's will to manage the scandal and preserve his own reputation, whatever the cost. "No one in his right mind will agree to it."

He smiled thinly. "Then you need not concern yourself about the indignity."

I swallowed hard and then pasted a smile onto my mouth. "Fine. But if that's the way it's going to be, the least you can do is buy us new shoes."

"I'll see to it."

I went into the hall, feeling a sense of vague disquiet. I had to get control of this situation somehow. But before I could think of anything, a muffled voice called my name.

"Gemma."

I knew the voice, and my heart stood painfully still. Then I pasted the smile back up and went to stand before a small oval mirror hanging near the stairs. "Doge?"

In the glass, he appeared just behind my reflection, adjusting the angle of a teardrop-shaped pearl hanging in one ear. The hair prickled on the back of my neck, but I resisted the urge to glance behind me. "I hope you won't miss another evening, Gemma."

"No, my lord. I won't."

"Make sure to pay your respects when you come. I have a private request to make." He dropped his hand and looked at me with lifted eyebrows. "Why, signorina, you look pale. Is something the matter?"

I shook my head with what I hoped was a less sickly

smile than it felt. "No, your serenity. Nothing's wrong."

Nothing but the nightmare feeling of being trapped in a shrinking cage.

Chapter 2.

I didn't tell the girls about Papa's plan. It seemed too ridiculous to work, and I didn't want to worry them about it. But I underestimated Papa's knowledge of the world. At sundown, he knocked on the door of our room and let himself in, together with a man who looked nearly old enough to be Papa's own father. Behind them both came a manservant carrying a valise and then Maria, with three new pairs of shoes in a basket.

My heart plunged. Lucia moved closer to me, and even Filippa shot me a nervous look.

"My daughters," Papa said to the old man. "This is Gemma. This is Filippa. And...this is Lucia. Lucia, this is Signor Zuan Friuli."

As Lucia rose from her curtsey, she slipped a timid hand into mine. I avoided her glance. Friuli? The name was noble, but the man was decrepit. My stomach churned. This was exactly what had once frightened me.

Papa couldn't mean it. He *couldn't* have promised Lucia to this horrible old man.

He did mean it: "Signor Friuli will be spending the night

in the next room. Maria will chaperone." A second door led from our bedchamber into another which we'd often used as a sitting-room. Papa threw it open, beckoning Friuli after him. "I hope the arrangements are to your liking, signor."

Friuli and his manservant followed Papa into the next room. Both my sisters stared at me. "Gemma?" Filippa's face was undisguised disgust. "What on earth?"

Lucia shivered. "Did you see the way he looked at me?"

I pressed my knuckles against my mouth. "Oh *ciel!*"

"Don't, Gemma! You're frightening me. Why did Papa single me out like that?" Lucia's eyes were even wider than usual.

I dropped my voice to a whisper. "Because if anyone can find out where we go at night, Papa's promised to let him marry Lucia."

I thought for a moment that Lucia would faint. Filippa paled. "That old goat?"

"I didn't believe he'd actually do it! I didn't believe anyone would be interested!"

Lucia sat down on the end of our bed and stared at me. I swallowed. "I'm sorry. I should have warned you."

"What are we going to do?" she whispered.

Filippa planted her hands on her hips. "Easy! We stay put and wait for him to give up."

On the other side of the room Maria finished putting our new shoes into a chest, folded her hands, and stood watching us with inscrutable face. Till now, I'd often found the presence of a chaperone comforting, a guarantee that I didn't have to bother speaking to men I didn't like. It struck me for the first time that not just princes but also prisoners are kept by guards.

"We can't wait." I pulled Filippa closer, lowering my voice again so that Maria wouldn't hear. "The Doge wants to see me tonight."

"Say you can't. You managed it last night."

"And he wasn't happy." I shook my head. "We can't risk it."

I saw the flicker of fear in her eyes. The Glass Doge might be our only temporary escape from the palazzo, but evidently both of us understood how dangerous he might turn out to be.

Papa came back into our room, alone. Lucia got up, clasping her hands together. "Papa," she said in a tiny, miserable voice.

He only looked more forbidding. "I'm sorry, Lucia. There's no other choice."

Behind him, Signor Friuli silently shuffled into the doorway. We all fell silent under the unblinking glitter of his eyes. I shivered.

"Well." Papa spoke with false cheerfulness. "Shall we dine, signor?"

When they were gone, Lucia burst into tears.

Filippa put her arms around Lucia and glared at me. "This is *your* fault, Gemma! What's going to happen to us now?"

41

She was right. It was my fault. If I hadn't left the palazzo last night—

No. If Papa had spoken to me, I wouldn't have *needed* to leave the palazzo.

"No, it isn't," I said fiercely. "It isn't my fault. It's all Papa's fault. All of it."

That only made Lucia cry harder.

"But I'm going to take care of it. Never fear." I glanced around the room, looking for some inspiration. *Mirror, communicating door, Maria...*

"Maria." I crooked my finger at the slave. "I have an errand for you."

* * *

Night fell. In our big canopied bed, I kept watch with the curtain pinched aside, listening to my sisters breathe unevenly in the darkness. Filippa, in the middle, kept shifting restlessly. Beyond her, Lucia still gave the occasional sniffle.

We always kept a lighted taper next to the bed. None of us, least of all me, liked the idea of lying in the dark with the mirror yawning from the wall. From the bed, I could watch both it and the open door that communicated with Signor Friuli's room. In the dark, I could just trace the dark shape of the bed in the next room, its curtains still open. Was the old man still awake, still keeping his vigil?

My gut churned. Old men married young girls often

enough that the fear had driven me to leave the palazzo to see the man Papa intended for me. But to think of it happening to Lucia made my guts boil. I ought to have protected her from this.

I *would* protect her from this.

On Lucia's side of the bed, Maria had slipped sideways in her high-backed chair and was snoring steadily. I'd had her bring me Mama's medicine-chest and a cup of wine. The chest was well stocked with the laudanum pills which Mama depended on for her sleep, and once Maria was out of the room again, it didn't take long to grind one to powder and add it to the winecup.

"You're going to drug him?" Lucia had whispered. "But we can't do that! Can we?"

"Watch me."

"But is that *right?*"

"Is it right to set a creepy old man to watch us? Is it?" I'd parried. And, of course, she had made no reply.

I couldn't help wondering what they'd say if they knew that the Glass Doge also watched us. And that it was my fault.

When Maria returned from settling Mama, I had her take the drugged wine to the next room. To our dismay, she returned at once bearing the full cup. "The signor thanks you, but he's drunk enough wine tonight, signorina."

Plague! But as one plan perished, a second presented itself. "You might as well drink it yourself, Maria."

43

It was good wine, and she didn't suspect me. She drank it down and took her place in her chair, propping her feet on a stool with a sigh of relief. Within minutes, she was snoring.

"But what about Signor Friuli?" Lucia had whispered.

"I'll think of something," I told her. In truth, I already had an idea so desperate I knew I could never tell them.

Only I would bear the guilt for this. As I lay in bed waiting, I went over the plan again and again in my mind. It would depend on close timing and careful management. But I would make it work. I had no other choice.

I was watching the mirror when the eyes of the gorgon head glowed golden for a brief moment and then faded.

The taper by our bed muttered in a gust of cold air.

My sisters did not move, lying as if spellbound. Aware of the open door, it took a mental effort to push back the covers and slip between the curtains, but my sisters followed when I did. In order to dress, we clustered against the wall that divided our room from Signor Friuli's, the wall that bore the mirror, where no one watching would see us.

Stays. Stockings. Gowns. Shoes, new and sleek with their glass beads winking complacently in the candlelight.

There was no sound from the next room, and I thought that perhaps my hopes were rewarded: perhaps Friuli had indeed fallen asleep. But as Lucia pinned a strand of pearls across the back of my hair, we all heard the bedstead creak.

"He's *watching* us," Lucia whispered, close to tears again.

"I know."

Filippa gave a hiss of annoyance and snatched the pins from Lucia's hand, jabbing them cruelly into my scalp. "Quick, or he'll see us leave!"

I turned, grabbing her wrist. "Wait."

She dropped her whisper to the merest breath of sound. "He's going to follow us, Gemma."

"I know," I said again.

I took the taper from our bedside and carried it to the mirror. The surface appeared foggy, as if the room had become suddenly very cold. My reflection blurred and softened. A chill breath of air raised bumps on my skin.

I reached out my hand.

Cold slid over my fingers like water. I ducked my head and stepped over the gold frame, right through the glass and out on the other side.

The bedroom beyond was the very image of our own bedroom, but reversed. Now I was facing the door that led out to the hall and the stairs. Beyond the glass, this house was cold, its windows broken and the tattered furnishings rippling in the fitful night air. But the mirrors were the same, and I knew if I went to them, I would look out at the different rooms and doings of our own palazzo.

I shivered. Passage through the glass always chilled me to the bone.

My sisters stepped through and stood beside me.

"Don't look back," I whispered.

We stole into the portego and took the echoing stairs down through the empty palazzo. The only light in this place shone from my flickering taper. There was no Papa in the study. No servants washing dishes in the kitchen. And the front door stood half open upon the grimy steps that led to the water.

I'd only ventured out into the streets of Venice once. But I'd danced a hundred times in the city beyond the glass.

Above us, a stair creaked.

"He's following us!" Lucia squeaked.

"Let him."

"But the Glass Doge—"

"I told you I'd think of something." I lifted my candle, shielding it from the cold wind with my hand, and stepped through the front door.

The Grand Canal stretched left and right along an arcade of dark, dead palazzos. Some had already slipped into the water, leaving only piles of rubble behind them. Others stood with their lower floors and arches swamped in lagoon-water. Beyond the glass, only one house was lit and cared for; only one house echoed to the strains of music.

The palazzo facing us across an empty canal glowed like a lonely lantern. Somehow, its solitary spark of life just made the rest of the city seem more silent and dead by comparison. I couldn't help thinking of the Venice I had seen last night, how much more living and bright and wonderful it had been.

I lifted the candle and shifted my protecting hand to let a gleam escape. The signal was seen. Three dark gondolas left their mooring-poles opposite and drifted toward us.

The Glass Doge always sent three boats to carry each of us separately. The first gondola kissed the steps, and the gondolier bowed and offered his hand to help me in. Then he dipped his oar in the water, and the gondola skimmed toward the palazzo opposite.

I looked back. Filippa was already climbing into the second boat. Behind her, Lucia stood with one hand crushing the satin of her skirt and the other pinching her lower lip, looking over her shoulder into the dark house.

She didn't have long to wait; a third gondola nosed its way to the steps to collect her. Behind it, a fourth slid into place, awaiting Signor Friuli.

As always, the Doge knew how many boats to send.

My gondola bumped the step of the Doge's house. I lifted my hem and stepped up onto the threshold. The door was open, and the light of a thousand candles streamed out, bright as day.

I handed my cloak to the footman at the door. Inside, the portego was a press of chattering people in Carnival masks. Overhead, the flourish of music and the tramp of feet told me that the dancing had already begun.

My sisters joined me. Lucia still looked nervous. "Look." She tugged on my sleeve, and I followed her gaze back across the canal to where the fourth gondola had

47

just moved away from the steps of our palazzo. Friuli.

"For the love of heaven, stop worrying!" I shook her hand off my arm. "Just enjoy yourself and be ready to leave quickly and quietly when I call you, all right? I have to speak to the Doge."

I was halfway to the staircase when someone said, "Gemma!"

I clapped a hand to my slamming chest and turned, but it was only Pollonia. We went by our Christian names here, so I did not know what family she came from, or what station she was on the other side of the glass. Sometimes, I suspected her of being low-born. But her dress was always respectable.

She leaned forward, brushing the lips of her mask against the cheek of mine. Her eyes crinkled with mischief. "You've been *followed*, my dear. The Doge will be happy with you."

I glanced at the door. Old Friuli climbed onto the doorstep, gaping at the party inside. A footman relieved him of his cloak and bowed, motioning him further in.

My sisters had vanished, probably hiding among the crowd. "I can't talk now, Pollonia. Do you know where the Doge is?"

"Upstairs. Where else?" She slipped her arm through mine and tugged me toward the stair. I always felt reluctant to let the girls out of my sight, but they knew not to do anything foolish—or at least Filippa did.

Probably better than I did myself.

"Pollonia." I knew I'd said I didn't have time to talk, but I had to know. "The first time I came here, you warned me to cross through the glass again before dawn."

Pollonia's eyes flashed white and quizzical in her black mask as she glanced in my direction.

I swallowed. "What happens if you don't make it in time?"

I had the feeling that she was on her guard. "You stay," she whispered after a moment.

"But you could go home the following evening, couldn't you?"

She shook her head. "No. You *stay*. You become part of the Glass City. That's the Doge's privilege, you understand."

The hair prickled on the back of my neck, but deep down, I felt only hot and angry gladness.

Good.

"Do you know anyone who…" I tried to think of the right phrase. *Decided to stay? Got trapped?*

Pollonia didn't look my way. "Yes." She dropped her voice "Everyone, sooner or later. Your sisters are sweet girls, Gemma. Don't…"

She went rigid. I followed her gaze to the top of the stair where the Glass Doge came toward us with his hands extended and the candlelight winking on his jet buttons and iron-grey hair.

"Gemma!" His voice was warm as sunlight. "My dear, I've been waiting for you. Come up, come up."

He paid not the slightest attention to Pollonia as he gently unhooked our arms—as if Pollonia was suddenly incapable of moving of her own accord—and led me up the stair himself. As we reached the top, I heard a little gasp and looked back to see Pollonia turn away, holding the rail and putting a hand to her stomacher as if something pained her.

The Doge led me through heavy double doors into the ballroom. This took up most of one floor of the whole palazzo. Tonight, as always, it blazed with light reflected from a hundred different surfaces, all smooth and mirror-bright. Overheard, enormous paintings were set into the ceiling. I didn't know who had painted them, but there must have been twenty or thirty of them. At first glance, they seemed to display scenes from Venice's history, but the closer I looked, the less certain I'd become. There was something faintly wrong with each of them. There were the familiar compositions suggesting the rediscovery of Saint Mark, or the meeting of the Pope and the Emperor, but in each case the figures were wrong; all of them revolved, somehow, around the tall nobleman with the iron-grey hair.

There was no doubt who was the spider at the centre of this web.

Lines of dancers advanced, turned, clapped and circled through the motions of the dance. All of them were masked; that was one of the unspoken rules here. Here, only the Glass Doge showed his true face. The city beyond the glass was cut off from the daylight Venice; it was the dark side of the city, the place where you could be anyone for a few hours. Where all obligations and duties, all contracts and agreements were erased.

In the Daylight City, they said that God had placed each man in his station, and that to change it was an act of sacrilege repugnant to the order of the cosmos itself. No wonder so many of us came here at night, if the Glass Doge offered something that God himself would not.

The Doge bent down to speak into my ear. "Now, Gemma. Do you remember the little discussion we had on your first visit?"

"Please, not here." I glanced behind and met Filippa's eyes as she and Lucia came to the top of the stair. "Can't we go somewhere private?"

The Doge observed my sisters and my discomfort. He arched a black eyebrow. "They don't know?"

The first time my sisters and I had discovered where our mirror led, the Doge took me aside to tell me that there was a price for dancing in his palazzo. One day, he would claim a favour in return.

The way he'd put it, there was nothing to worry about. I'd agreed without thinking, eager to taste this new freedom. But the moment the words had crossed my lips, I'd begun to wonder what that favour might be, and whether it was going to be something I could pay with honour.

The more I'd worried, the less I'd felt like telling my

sisters.

"Is it necessary they should know? I'd rather not concern them in this." I swallowed. "If you have any requests to make, your serenity, you can make them to me."

"As you like it." The Doge pressed my arm a little closer and crossed through the double line of dancers. Without looking our way, they parted and flowed around us like water, as if sensing the Doge's presence with something other than sight. Beyond, the far wall was lined with gilt-framed mirrors. I had a sudden disconcerting vision of a man in black and a girl in white rushing toward me. Then the chill of glass slipped around me. And then the Doge dropped my hand, and we stood in a vast, cold room of crumbling plaster and bare lath. Blue moonlight shone through the ornate iron grille of the window before me, but warm gold blazed from the ballroom behind.

I turned, letting go of the Doge's arm. Through the frail curtain of glass behind me it was possible to hear the muffled music, to see the dancing.

The Doge touched my upswept hair. "I like it better down."

My skin crawled, the way it always did when I remembered how closely I was watched. Every minute of every day.

I adjusted my face and looked up at him with a smile. "Is that your request, then, Doge? Easily granted."

He laughed silently and removed his hand. "Oh no,

signorina. And what I ask is less a request and more a...price."

"A price?" I screwed up my lips, half terrified to be alone with him in this room, half terrified of what he was about to ask and wanting to put off the moment as long as I could. "I thought we left all that sort of thing behind us in the Daylight City."

"Ah, but you did. You came here for something you could have only if you hid your face and forgot your past. For freedom." The Doge was silent for a moment. "In the Daylight City, you gain what you give. You inherit what you lay up. You reap what you sow. Here beyond the glass, those rules don't apply. But first, to escape the Daylight City, there is a price... I can offer you freedom in everything but this."

The more he spoke, the more my heart sank. "Why, though?" If the Glass Doge was powerful enough to break the cycle of spend-and-get that had Venice so tightly bound, why should I have to pay for my visits beyond the glass?

"It takes a very great deal of power to open so many mirrors." The Doge passed his finger through the glass. "Power that must be sustained, in part, by the presence of many...*living* things."

Power? Say magic, rather. The skin prickled on my neck. I shouldn't listen to this. If the Inquisitors ever asked... I should leave now. I should stay away.

I should never have come.

I licked my lips. "And the price?"

"I require an exchange." He shifted his shoulder with half an apologetic smile. "Tawdry, I know. But what can one do? The whole world becomes more like a city each day. Your presence here with your sisters every night is not enough to cover the opening of your mirror." He hesitated. "I need lives."

I opened my mouth to object. I had never agreed to this.

But I had. Like a fool, before I knew what I was promising.

"Lives." I marvelled at the steadiness of my own voice. "In exchange for..."

"Yours, of course." He inclined his head in a slight bow. "Nothing terrible, I assure you! A simple ransom. Their life for yours. Their freedom for yours. You need only find me three people to come and remain here beyond the glass. Or four, rather, since tonight you've brought a friend."

"He's not our friend!" The warmth I'd felt in the ballroom faded away, leaving me shivering in the cold February draughts of the empty room. Three lives against my freedom, my sisters' freedom. I shouldn't have come here. A magic mirror, Gemma, really? In what story did meddling with such things ever come to any good?

Maybe it would be better than the convent, though. Two of us would go to the convent in any case. Perhaps we'd be better off coming here instead. Or would we? I

54

knew what the Doge was, didn't I? Was I willing to risk my immortal soul?

The thoughts rebounded through my mind in chaos. "How long do I have?"

"A year and a day, dated from your first visit."

He sounded like a pepper merchant himself now. I bit back another complaint. Half the time was already gone. How would I ransom Filippa and myself?

It didn't matter. At least I already had a way to ransom one of us.

At least I knew he deserved it.

"You can have Friuli."

"His full name?" the Doge inquired gravely.

"Zuan Friuli." I wrapped my arms around myself, trying to bring some warmth to my shivering body. "He can be Lucia's ransom."

"For Lucia," he repeated with a formal bow. "Mind he does not follow you back through the mirror by dawn. And mind you bring me two more before the year and a day are ended. Unless you'd prefer to remain yourself."

I glanced up, hearing the greedy note in his voice, seeing the glitter in his eyes. There was a lust here every bit as insatiable as old Friuli's. Not for the same thing, of course. The Doge relished my fear more than my youth and beauty.

"If I do it, if I bring you two more exchanges, then we don't have to keep coming here. We can stay home. Can't we?"

"Why, Gemma, don't you enjoy our company?"

"Please just answer me, Doge."

"You are always free to do as you wish, Gemma."

"But there will be no more obligations after this."

He hesitated, as if the word cost him. "None."

The tension in my shoulders unstitched. "Then I'll bring you two more exchanges."

Of course I agreed to it. You would have done the same.

* * *

I tried to dance. I tried to enjoy myself.

I told myself that something would turn up. I had six months left, after all. That was a long time. I could find a different way to pay the Doge's price—or maybe I would find someone for whom a life beyond the glass would be welcome. Someone who had never known luxury or leisure.

But how? I spent my waking hours locked in the palazzo. With Mama so ill and unable to chaperone us, we rarely had the chance to leave. And when we did, under the watchful eye of whatever servant or distant relative Papa could find to accompany us, there was never a chance to stop and speak to anyone—let alone canal brats and beggars.

If the Doge insisted on being paid in lives, did that mean that half the people here never left? I scrutinised the people around me with new curiosity. The short plump girl in the grey-and-silver, the tall willowy brunette in the white-and-green, the stocky man opposite me: how many of them were doomed to pass the rest of their lives here?

I found I couldn't fake cheerfulness. When the music stopped, Pollonia was standing behind me. "You seem so quiet tonight, Gemma."

I pulled her into an empty alcove. "Pollonia. How many of the people here are…"

She tried to pull free of me. "Don't…"

I gripped tighter. Spoke in a whisper. "Are *you*?"

She didn't answer, but I was close enough to see the answer in her dark brown eyes. "I can't *say*, Gemma."

It struck me that I had never seen anyone but ourselves entering or leaving the Doge's palazzo. Could it really be all of them?

I let go, half expecting her to flee. Instead, she stood motionless, as if trying to make some decision.

"Listen, Gemma. You can't…"

I interrupted her. "How long has it been?"

A hesitation. "Too long."

"What is it like?"

It was impossible to see much of her expression under the mask she wore, but her eyes were elaborately blank. "Marvellous. It's marvellous. I love it here."

"Fine." But I tasted bitter misgiving. I couldn't risk losing my sisters to this place. Could I really hand over Friuli?

Pollonia saw I wouldn't pursue the matter, and her shoulders slackened. "Fine, then." She nodded behind me. "Who's your guest?"

I glanced in the direction of her nod. Lucia sat not far away and next to her, old Friuli leaned close, speaking too low for me to hear over the murmur of voices in the room. I couldn't see Lucia's face, but I could read her uncomfortable posture.

"Plague him!" I spat. "Pollonia, you have to help us. Otherwise, Papa is going to force Lucia to marry that man." I grabbed her arm. "The Doge said that if we got back through the glass without him following us, Friuli will stay here. Please…"

I couldn't help blushing at my own words. I half expected her to refuse. Even a flicker of disapproval, a dry mocking laugh, and who knows if I might have turned back, even after giving my word to the Doge?

Instead, she shot me a look of sympathy. "I'll take care of it, Gemma."

"You will?"

"You and I are women and therefore sisters. I know what it's like to be used as a bargaining-piece between selfish men."

She squeezed my shoulder and slipped through the crowd in Friuli's direction.

I had danced only twice more when Filippa and Lucia appeared next to my elbow. "Shouldn't we go?" Filippa whispered. "It's grey in the east."

I'd barely seen them all night; they had sidled to and fro in the room, the mice to Friuli's cat, silently but constantly avoiding him. It filled my mouth with bile to think of my sisters exposed to such attentions. It filled my heart with no less dread to think of leaving them here under the Doge's eye, his subtle taste for cruelty.

I was willing to contemplate enduring either Friuli or the Doge for myself. But I could not, I *would* not allow my sisters to suffer.

I scanned the large ballroom until I spotted Friuli sitting in an alcove with Pollonia, one arm around her waist, eating raisins from her hand like a fool a fraction of his age. He didn't see me, but Pollonia did. First she grimaced, and then she blew me a stealthy kiss.

"Yes," I said. "Let's go."

Linking hands, we slipped our way through the crowd and down the stairs. The door of the palazzo stood open onto water that was now tinged with silver in the predawn light. It was already later than I had thought. As I signalled to the gondoliers, Lucia tugged my arm.

"Gemma? What about Signor Friuli?"

Plague! "Let him find his own way back."

"What if he doesn't? He has to get back through the mirror before dawn, doesn't he?"

"Ciel, Lucia, there's no time! We're late enough as it is."

I twitched my skirt from between her fingers and stepped into the gondola. In my haste, it rocked alarmingly, and I lurched into the seat with a grab for the

59

gunwale.

"Gemma," Lucia squeaked as we shot away from the doorstep.

Next to Lucia, Filippa hadn't said a word. She threw an undecided glance from me to Lucia, from Lucia to the Doge's house. As Lucia caught her arm and asked a question, Filippa looked worried. But then her own gondola kissed the step, and she looked east and shrugged, and stepped into the boat.

I let out a sigh of relief. Filippa sometimes stood up to me, it was one of the reasons I respected her, but I knew Lucia lacked the courage to oppose us both. Sure enough, my youngest sister stood indecisively on the step only long enough for the third gondolier to halt before her. Then with one last anxious glance behind, she stepped into the boat.

When I reached the step of the palazzo that mirrored our own in the Daylight City, I didn't wait on the step for the others. Instead, I hurried upstairs, pulling the mask from my face. On the third floor, the mirror's surface was still soft and misty. But the grey light of dawn grew stronger every moment.

Filippa and Lucia followed me into the room. "He's not following us," Lucia panted. "What will happen, Gemma?"

"I don't know." A lie, but I could think of nothing better. "Come on." I braced myself and plunged through the mist.

In the Daylight City, the door between our room and Friuli's was still open and Maria was still fast asleep in her chair.

As Filippa and Lucia followed me, I put my finger to my lips to warn them against waking her. In perfect silence, we stripped off our finery and unpinned our hair. I was standing in the centre of the room with an armful of gowns and stays when Maria stopped snoring and shifted in her chair. Swiftly, I bundled the clothing under the bed.

The slave sat up, rubbing sleep from her eyes and yawning at the three of us in our rumpled shifts. Then her eyes widened and she rose groggily to her feet. "Is it morning? Already?"

Was the mirror still open? What if, at this final moment, Maria discovered our secret? I didn't dare look. But Filippa and Lucia both turned to glance at the mirror.

"It's dawn," Filippa said, and the tension drained from my shoulders. We were safe. The mirror was closed. Friuli was trapped. And Maria, still vague and unsteady from her drugged sleep, hadn't even noticed my sisters' guilty looks.

"*Santi angeli,*" Maria muttered. "I slept all night. The signor will have my skin." Still muttering, she rubbed sleep from her slitted eyes and shuffled across to the door which led to Signor Friuli's room. I think she meant to close it to allow us to dress. Instead, she hesitated on the threshold. "Signor?"

She pushed the door wide and went in. The bed beyond was rumpled but empty.

61

"Signor?" Maria asked again. Louder. Alarmed. Then she came back to our room with her brow wrinkled in puzzlement. "Gone," she said in her harsh voice, locking the door.

She also locked our door as she went to find Papa. I bundled the clothes out from under the bed again and started to lay them away with shaking fingers.

My sisters stared at me anxiously.

I know what you're thinking: *How did you not foresee this, Gemma?* The truth is, I'd been so completely swallowed up by the problem of saving Lucia that it had never occurred to me to wonder what would happen in the morning when Friuli had vanished without a trace.

I never was very good at chess.

Lucia looked from me to Filippa. "Is he going to come back?"

"Oh, San Marco, I hope not!" Filippa burst out. "Horrible man!"

"What are you so worried about?" I snapped. "If he wasn't so busy trying to tickle Pollonia, he'd be safely back by now, telling Papa all about the glass city. Do you *want* to marry him? Do you *want* Filippa and me sent back to Saint Mary?"

Lucia swallowed. "No. I just…"

"Just stop worrying! Everyone's got what they want. That horrible Friuli has Pollonia to amuse him, you don't have to marry him, and Filippa and I don't have to go to a nunnery."

62

And the Doge has his first permanent guest.

"Except Papa," Filippa said.

"Excuse me?"

"Papa doesn't have what he wants."

A son-in-law.

As if he knew we were speaking of him, the door banged open and Papa strode in. "What do you mean, gone?" he said tightly. Maria followed him. After her came Friuli's valet, wringing his hands and clucking like a frightened hen. Papa fumbled with the lock to the guest room, swearing under his breath. My sisters clustered a little closer.

Papa got the door open. The valet rushed in, volubly upset, but Papa saw at once that the room was empty. Instantly, he turned his attention to us.

"I take it you know exactly what happened here last night."

I gripped Lucia's wrist warningly. "Why don't you ask Maria?" I challenged him. "She was supposed to be watching us."

Maria was inside Friuli's room with the valet, looking under the bed and throwing open the chests. "Oh yes, and what will Maria tell me?" Papa asked sarcastically. "That she fell asleep? Or that you all rode off on broomsticks?"

Plague. She might indeed accuse us of some ghastly misdeed sooner than risk Papa's wrath by confessing to having fallen asleep. Not that the truth was any better. My stomach knotted.

63

Papa's lips firmed. "Right now, I'm not sure which I'd find more credible."

We were interrupted by the return of the servants. The valet declared that his master would never leave the palazzo without his servant, without his valise... He was owed two months' wages. It was a shameful trick. He would complain to the Heads of the Sestieri.

Papa shooed them into the hall and came back to stare at us. "This is no laughing matter." He rarely raised his voice when he was angry, and although he spoke softly now, I'd never seen him more furious. "A citizen of the Republic has vanished in my house. If he cannot be found within a day or two, the Republic will hear of it. What did you do with him?"

Lucia and Filippa looked at me.

I swallowed. "Nothing." It was, strictly speaking, no lie. My sin was one of omission.

"Do you know where he is?"

"No, signor." That was also, strictly, no lie. I could not have pointed out Signor Friuli's location on any map. I did not even know for certain that he was where I had last seen him.

"I *will* have the truth." Papa went out, slamming the door behind him.

Filippa must have seen the fear in my face. "Gemma? What have you done?"

"*Nothing, Filippa!*"

"We should just tell him," Lucia whispered.

"We *can't.*" I swallowed, lowering my voice. "Don't you realise? We should never have gone through that mirror at all. Now, we're beholden to the Doge—but if anyone ever finds out, if the Inquisitors get wind of this, we won't be just locked up in a nunnery. We'll be *dead.*"

There was a long, awful silence.

"What happens if there's another suitor?" Filippa whispered.

I had no answer for that. None that I was willing to admit, at any rate. "We'll worry about that when it happens," I said. And then, more grimly, "Pray that it doesn't."

* * *

But it did happen, and it happened before nightfall.

There was nothing to do in the palazzo, nothing to keep me from running in endless circles on the treadmill of my worries. At least in the convent we'd had lessons, lacework, and prayers to keep us occupied.

There was one thing I hadn't been able to do in the convent. The day was unseasonably clear, and the other girls spoke of bleaching one's hair in the sun. I found a crownless sun-hat and went downstairs to find lemon-juice, but as I descended the stair through the piano nobile, I heard voices in Papa's study.

I peeked around the corner and looked across the portego directly in at the open door and into Papa's eyes.

"Gemma!" He beckoned.

As I obeyed, the man standing before Papa's desk turned to glance at me. *Man?* This was no more than a boy, a gangling lad with curling hair and spots.

For the moment, Papa ignored me. To the boy, he said, "I ought to warn you: there may be risks."

"I understand that, signor."

I'd assumed he was a new suitor, come to try his luck at Papa's wager. But as he twisted a velvet bonnet nervously between his fingers, I noticed how knobbly and scarred his hands were. A tradesman? But a match between patrician and plebeian was not just unheard-of, it was forbidden by law.

Maybe the scars were come by in a brawl.

Papa frowned. "I might as well be honest with you. There was another…applicant…last night. This morning he had vanished. His servants are at a loss. It's possible he may have left the palazzo, fallen afoul of some ruffians in the alleys, or…" A helpless gesture. "It seems he has interests in Padua. He may yet be found, but…"

The hands tightened on the bonnet. "I understand, signor."

"I've faced danger before." The new voice made me jump as I realised there was a fourth person in the room, sitting before Papa's desk in a wooden chair with a high carved back that concealed him from me. "I think ruffians in any alley would find it difficult to deal with me, Signor Caloprini."

That voice! I knew I'd heard it before, but I couldn't remember where. I inched to one side, trying to catch a glimpse of the occupant.

Meanwhile, the boy cleared his throat. "Whatever the danger, I'm willing to try it, Signor Caloprini." His jaw firmed and it made him look even younger, but very earnest. My heart sank. *Liking* was the last thing I wanted to feel for any of Papa's candidates. "And with all respect to this gentleman, I came here before he did."

Papa's eyes flickered to the hands. "What did you say your name was, signor? Benito Mafei? The name is familiar, but not at the Council."

"We're glassworkers, signor. My father's had the privilege of trading with you."

So I was right: he was in trade, handling hot glass. Papa frowned. On one hand, the Murano glassworkers were the next best thing to nobility in Venice, the only class permitted to marry into the patriciate. On the other, while it was common for patrician men to marry beneath themselves for the sake of money, none of the truly great houses would ever give a daughter to a family of less rank than themselves.

The real reason so many of us were locked into convents was not law, was not expense or necessity. It was pure devilish pride.

Papa spoke slowly: "Salvator Mafei, is that right? We've sent several shipments of his glass to France. Fine work, but…" But not the kind of family the Caloprinis would make alliance with.

The boy reached eagerly into his tunic and pulled out a sealed paper. "He sends you this, signor, and begs you to read it."

In silence, Papa broke the seal, unfolded the paper, and took his time in reading it. I tried to construe his face, hoping for signs of displeasure. This boy gave me a hollow feeling in the pit of my stomach. Papa had to send him away.

It seemed an age before he lowered the paper and removed his spectacles. "What happens if you also disappear, Messer Benito?"

The boy swallowed, and his reserve cracked. "I've spoken to Signorina Lucia before, signor. I would brave *any* risks for her."

Plague, plague, *plague!* I tried to catch Papa's eye, to shake my head.

Ignoring me, Papa lifted an ironic eyebrow. "I see. But your father suggests…if I read correctly what he *doesn't* say…that if I should fail to accept your application, no more Mafei glass contracts will be forthcoming. He also says you're his only son and best workman. Pardon me, but if something happens to you in my house, I fear I won't just lose the Mafei contracts; I'll be dragged into the Doge's interrogation chamber."

Benito straightened. "My father has emancipated me. I'm my own man and I'm willing to take the risk. Will you accept me if I ask him not to penalise you for any failure of mine?"

Papa was evidently impressed. Most fathers didn't emancipate their sons at such a young age. Many even remained minors in their father's house long after marriage; some were never emancipated until their father's death.

"It's too risky, Papa," I blurted out as he drew breath to speak.

He shot me a quelling look, and I realised that by voicing my opinion, I'd only strengthened his resolve. "I will allow it, Messer Benito. I've passed my word that anyone of eligible status who can discover where my daughters go at night will marry one of them." He rang for a servant and turned to the man in the high-backed chair, who'd been so quiet, I'd almost forgotten about him. "I'm sorry, Signor Gonzaga."

Gonzaga. I mouthed the word in shock. The man in the alley, who'd mistaken me for a harlot and then left me to die.

The stranger in the wooden chair stood up and bowed to Papa. "No hard feelings, signor. I'll call again tomorrow morning." He turned to Benito. "Let Fortune favour the brave, my friend." And then he turned again and came face to face with me.

Papa cleared his throat. "My eldest daughter."

Unmasked, Gonzaga was not quite as old as I'd guessed; he had to be around thirty, squint-lines scored around his eyes and a perpetual twist in the corner of his mouth.

69

"Signorina," he said, reaching out for my hand.

I backed away and put both my hands behind me.

The cynical twist at the corner of his mouth grew deeper. Then he bowed and passed us, and a servant showed him out.

"Messer Benito, my eldest daughter Gemma," Papa shot me a look that warned me to behave. I pressed my lips together and curtseyed. Maybe it would be best for all of us if I found a way to scare this boy off.

But if Papa's awful hints didn't put him off, what could?

Papa rang the bell for Maria. "Take Messer Benito and introduce him to your sisters. And, Gemma." He leaned forward, his eyes suddenly pleading, his voice dropping lower. "Don't forget that you can end this at any time. Just by confessing."

"I'll remember." I avoided looking at the young man beside me. *Oh, Papa. If only it were that simple.*

* * *

"Did you know that he's not allowed to leave the lagoon?"

"Who?"

"Benito. It's the law. The glass trade is too valuable to the Republic, so none of the glassmakers can ever leave. And they can never teach the trade to foreigners either."

I didn't pay much attention to Lucia and Filippa's chatter. The three of us were having dinner in our own room, and Maria was attending to Mama, so I had taken

70

out another laudanum pill and was busy crushing it into another cup of wine.

Lucia watched me with concern. "Gemma?"

I waited for her to go on, but she seemed to be having trouble with the words.

"Gemma?"

"What are you waiting for, permission? For heaven's sake, say it."

"Gemma, we aren't going to leave Benito behind, are we?"

Benito. In one afternoon, the young glassmaker and my sister had progressed to Christian names. I still wasn't sure when he'd seen her before. Perhaps at one of the few parties we'd attended since leaving the convent. But I liked him so far. And worse, Lucia obviously liked him too.

"Leave him behind? Who said anything about leaving people behind? Friuli didn't get back to the mirror on time, that's all. He ought to have been more careful."

"We ought to have told him. We ought to tell him tonight."

I knew there was no use telling Signor Friuli anything now that he was trapped in the glass city. But I didn't want them to know what I had done, even for their sake.

"No, don't. At least not until this is over. Remember, if he gets back and tells Papa where we've been, then it will be the Inquisitors for all of us."

"The strappado," Filippa whispered under her breath.

Lucia turned pale.

The door in the next room opened, and Maria escorted Benito into it. "You watch from here," she told him in her harsh voice, "and the door stays open."

She came through into our room, and Benito followed her until he stood in the open doorway. Shyly, he looked into Lucia's eyes.

"I wish there was some other way, signorina."

As she looked at him, her lips parted, but only a tiny sigh emerged.

He was obviously too tongue-tied to continue. "Forgive me." He backed away from the door.

"Wait." I jumped up. "Will you have some wine?"

"No, thank you, signorina. Wine makes me sleepy."

He backed into his room and we heard the bed creak as he sat down on it. I clenched my jaw. *No. No, Benito, don't make me do this.*

I offered the cup to Maria. "You drink it, then."

She touched her tongue to her lips and shook her head. "No, signorina."

She knew what I'd done last night, then. Probably, Papa had scolded her not to repeat the mistake. If she refused the wine, if she stayed awake, she would find out where we went at night—and this dangerous dance would be done with.

But she was a slave, not a suitor, and I had more options when it came to Maria. I lowered my voice. "Drink it, Maria, or I'll tell Mama..." I had to think of some way of making her do what I wanted. But with what could you threaten a slave? There was only one thing bad enough, one thing commonplace enough to be credible. I pulled her aside, where my sisters couldn't hear us, and put my lips against her ear. "Drink it, or I'll tell Mama that Papa has had you in his room at night."

I could tell I had frightened her. Almost, I frightened myself. Maria stared at me with her cheeks gradually becoming the colour of yellow clay.

"Don't look so terrified." I glanced at my sisters, fearing that my fragile web of silence and half-truths would break. "Look cheerful and drink the wine, Maria."

I let go of her arm, but she went on staring at me. Had I ever bothered to look Maria in the eye before? For a moment I looked in at the windows of a house not much different to my own. Then she turned away and silently drank the wine.

I turned to find Filippa and Lucia watching us, concern and curiosity and unspoken fear on their faces. But it wasn't until we had shut the curtains around our bed and Maria lolled snoring in the chair beside us, that a whisper floated over to me from Filippa's side of the bed.

"What did you say to her, Gemma?"

"Nothing."

"She looked terrified."

Why must she be so much more difficult than Lucia? I didn't answer. Like last night, I had the edge of the curtain pulled aside. Benito had a candle burning in his room, and I could see him sitting on the foot of the bed with his feet drawn up on the edge of the mattress and his forehead propped on his knees.

"Is he watching us?" Lucia wanted to know.

"No. He's listening."

"I…" Lucia began.

"What?"

"Nothing."

Silence. I knew Lucia had something to say. It was clear that if we couldn't drug Benito, we'd have to trap him beyond the glass. I knew she didn't want me to do that. I knew she was too timid to say it.

Coward.

At last she took another breath. "We can bring them back whenever we want, can't we?"

"I hope so." But it was another lie.

Silence.

I let go of the curtain and turned over, staring into the darkness above. "Lucia, there may be no happy ending to this story. Look at it this way: if you had to choose which of us you'd never see again, your sisters or this pimply boy you've only just met, which would you pick?"

Her hand found its way into mine and squeezed it. "You, of course."

"So you trust me?"

"Of course I trust you."

I felt a little better about it. True, Lucia didn't know the real stakes. But if she did, she'd understand why Benito had to spend the rest of his nights in the city beyond the glass.

I peeked through the curtains again and glimpsed the mirror just at the moment of change, with the golden light just fading from the gorgon's eyes. "It's time." I raised my voice slightly: if Benito heard, so much the better. "The mirror's open."

We slipped out of bed. In his room, Benito stood up. "The mirror. The glass. Of course. They say the mirrors of Hieronimo the Old had strange powers…"

I looked at Filippa in surprise. Of course: the mirror must have come from Murano. Where else would a Venetian buy fine glass?

Filippa had an armful of stays and something else on her mind. She marched over to the communicating door. "We're getting dressed. We'll call you before we leave, word of honour," she said firmly, and closed the door.

I tightened Filippa's stays while Lucia tightened mine. The corded shell cinched my body, but there was a hollowness behind my breastbone that didn't occupy any physical space.

I'd only known Benito a single afternoon. I knew it would take much longer to *really* know him. But I couldn't imagine anyone who might be better for Lucia.

I thought of Gonzaga, waiting for his chance if Benito should fail. My stomach churned. Bitterness washed over me. As a male, Benito had had the kind of freedom I only dreamed about. Only sixteen, but he'd had all those years to explore a world that was denied me and my sisters. I would never have that. All I would have would be this palazzo, where I was ruled by Papa. The convent, where I was ruled by the Mother Superior. And the city beyond the glass, where the Glass Doge watched my every movement.

I left my hair down, the way the Doge preferred. When we were masked and ready, Lucia opened the communicating door, and Benito emerged with a cloak slung over his shoulders and his hand tapping eagerly on the hilt of his dagger.

We stepped through the mirror. As I led the way through the mirror palazzo and across the canal, Benito stayed by Lucia's side, staring and whispering. When we entered the downstairs vestibule of the Glass Doge's palazzo, he offered his arm to Lucia and led her upstairs to dance.

Filippa took hold of my arm with chilly fingers. "I hope you know what you're doing, Gemma."

More unanswerable questions. If she guessed so much, why didn't she guess that I had enough on my conscience without her help? "What do you mean?"

"Are you sure you can get him back?"

"Honestly, Filippa, that's the least of my worries." She might know about the Inquisitors, but she didn't know about the price demanded by the Glass Doge.

I turned away from her and climbed the stairs. In the crush of people at their head, I came face to face with

Signor Friuli.

I froze.

He was wearing a mask tonight, but there was no mistaking his small and shrivelled frame. He, too, recognised me. "Signorina Gemma?"

Before he could say anything else, I turned and elbowed my way into the crowd, heart pounding. I didn't stop until I was sure he couldn't see me. Under the mask, my cheeks were blazing hot. What was wrong with me? Why couldn't I look this detestable man in the eye?

What had I done that made me so much worse than him?

Someone moved to my side, and when I looked up, I saw the Glass Doge.

"I like your hair better this way." He wore a faint smile.

My mouth was dry, my heart still racing from my encounter with Friuli. If I waited, I would lose my nerve. "Doge, I've brought you another guest. Another to pay off our debt."

Behind the Doge, I could see dancers. Mirrors lined the far wall, doubling the apparent size of the room. Two identical crowds milled and supped, laughed and danced. Before my eyes, they melted and dislimned and ran together again. For the moment, all I saw was the Doge—dozens of Doges, a hundred Doges, a black-clad cloud of them. As if the room was nothing but mirrors, and one man was reflected in all of them.

Except that in the very midst of them, my sister Lucia,

a splash of white, danced with the glassblower's son.

Then I blinked, and the crowd was itself again. But my heart hammered as if I'd run all the way from the palazzo rooftop to the cellar and back again.

I didn't know what it meant, but it was sheerly terrifying, and I took an involuntary step back. The Doge waited, a half smile on his lips. I knew then, better than ever, that what I'd done was wrong. The Doge trapped people here, sucked the spirit from them, made them into images of himself.

Just like Papa did in the Daylight City.

I forced myself to harden. I'd done what I'd done to save Lucia from this. And for Filippa, I'd do it again.

"Tell me his name," said the Glass Doge.

"Benito Mafei. Take him and keep him. I do not think he will leave my sister if you give him the choice."

The Doge laughed soundlessly. "Accepted! But *you* must keep him from passing the glass before dawn."

"I'll do it. Just promise me there's no chance he or Friuli will ever leave."

"You have my word." The Doge bowed. The music came to an end, and the lines on the dancing-floor dissolved. Feeling suffocated by the perfumed heat, I pushed my way through the crowd and out onto the loggia that overlooked the canal.

Footsteps echoed behind me. The door shut with a snick. I turned to see Filippa take off her mask, her eyes a blue blaze of fury.

"What are you *doing*, Gemma?"

I blinked.

"He would be *perfect* for Lucia!" Her hands worked as she came toward me, and I thought she might actually hit me. "I heard what you said to the Doge! I feared they'd be trapped here forever—I never imagined you *knew!*"

Plague. No. "Filippa…"

She was in full spate. "That horrible old man, that was one thing. But Lucia would be *happy* with Benito. You could have made some deal with him. We could have come up with a story. We could have told Papa we sneak into Venice at night. Are you *really* frightened of the Inquisitors, Gemma? Or are you just trying to stay out of the convent?"

I laughed incredulously. "Ciel, Filippa, by this time I would almost be happy to see the convent again."

"Stop *lying* to us!" She folded her lips into a pale, stubborn line. "Someone has to tell him to get back through the mirror by dawn. It can be you, or it can be me. Take your pick."

"I've already promised him to the Doge."

It was the only excuse I could think of, but it didn't stop her. "Another lie. I *heard* what he said to you." She shook her head in scorn, and I knew I deserved it. "Fine. I'll tell him."

She turned away, reaching for the doorknob. Time fractured. I only had seconds to stop her.

"Are you willing to take his place, then?"

79

She looked back over her shoulder. "What?"

Now that she'd thrust herself into this mess, she was going to have to bear the blame with me. "I said, are you going to stay here instead of Benito? Because you'll have to."

She touched her tongue to her lips, her hand still hovering on the knob. "I don't understand."

I told her. I watched all the anger drain out of her, replaced by fear. My voice was miserable as I finished: "You said you wanted the truth. Well, now you have it."

Filippa pressed both hands against her mouth. "Ciel! Why didn't you tell us?"

I shrugged, suddenly close to tears. "Until last night, I didn't know the full price. You can't tell Lucia, Filippa. She'd die of worry."

"We should go home and smash the mirror. Now."

"You don't understand. It won't help. Don't you realise he sees everything we do? It's not just the gorgon mirror he watches us through, it's *all* of them. For six months I've lived in that house knowing that he sees every movement, hears every word. Speaks to me through the glass when you're not around."

"Oh ciel."

I took off my own mask and wiped my eyes. "You're right, Filippa. I shouldn't have led us into this. I shouldn't have given him this power over us. This is all my fault."

She shook her head. "There has to be *something* we can do."

80

"Pay the debt. It's the only way."

A convulsive swallow. "Benito," she whispered miserably.

"I paid Friuli for Lucia, and I'm paying Benito for you."

"And you? …Gemma?"

I shrugged. "I don't care about myself. Maybe I'll find someone else to pay for me. Maybe I'll just have to stay here. It doesn't matter." *Because I'm damned either way.*

"O Dio." Filippa whispered it like a prayer. "O Santa Maria, pray for us."

"I only wish she would."

Filippa closed her eyes. Her voice was only a terrified squeak when it came: "I don't want to stay here, Gemma!"

I couldn't speak.

"I only came because you made me. And someone had to take care of Lucia! I don't like such crowds of people. And I'm always so tired all the time. I—I could stand going back to the convent. It's peaceful."

I nodded miserably. On the day my sisters and I returned from Saint Mary of the Virgins, the day Papa announced he was seeking a match for me, he'd said much the same thing. I wasn't made for a convent. I needed people, excitement, and occupation. But although life in a convent would sometimes be hard for Lucia and Filippa, he said, it wouldn't be cruel.

There, I disagreed with Papa. It *was* cruel that so many of us should be locked up against our will, never to know love or pretty things except for what we could steal or smuggle.

But all my efforts to defy him had only resulted in worse trouble.

"Don't be afraid." I touched Filippa's shoulder comfortingly. "We'll pay our debt to the Doge. All this scandal will blow over and Lucia will marry the noblest of the noble—a Mocenigo or a Dandolo, not a citizen glassblower. And Papa will be so pleased he won't force us into a convent. Not unless we really want to."

Filippa reached up and took my hand. Tried to look hopeful. "Signor Friuli looks happy here. Maybe Benito will be too."

Damned either way, I thought. "Yes. Yes, he'll be happy."

This time she didn't accuse me of lying to her. That morning, I would lie awake wondering. Was it because she believed me? Or was it because she now preferred the lie to the truth?

Chapter 3.

I begin to think this house is bewitched, signor. I begin to think that this is a case for the Inquisitors."

Papa's desk was a mess. His books and papers lay in untidy, neglected heaps. The skin sagged under his eyes, making him look tired and truly old.

In the silence, I tried not to meet anyone's eyes.

The man named Gonzaga coughed very softly before he spoke. "That would be a shame, signor."

"For one man to vanish—that might be an accident. But two!" Papa lifted a despairing hand. "If I don't do something now, I'll risk falling afoul of the authorities myself."

With Filippa's help, it had been easy to trap Benito beyond the glass. Despite his obvious interest in my sister, Filippa and I had managed to decoy them away from each other. Then Pollonia had agreed to keep Benito dancing while the three of us sneaked across the canal and returned through the glass to the Daylight City.

Lucia had made no objection, but she hadn't spoken since. Not even once. Now, drooping in a corner of the study, she looked as defeated as Papa did.

"One moment, signor." Gonzaga tilted his head. "You'd report your own daughters to the Doge's tormentors? For witchcraft?"

"What else can I do?" Papa shot us an angry look. "I've tried commanding, begging, watching them... Maybe I *should* call the Inquisitors."

I exchanged a silent glance with Filippa. Her lips were white, but they remained shut.

Lucia only looked at the ground, her hands clasped as if she was praying.

"I don't believe that would profit either of us, signor." Gonzaga bent forward, pressing his palms together. "You need a solution, not a scandal. And I need a wife, not whatever's left once the Inquisitors are done with your daughters. Don't give up hope, Caloprini. Give me leave to solve this puzzle."

"Give you leave to vanish like the last two, you mean." Papa plucked at his beard. "This is *Venice*, not the mainland. We have a real government here. Venetian citizens can't vanish with no questions asked. If I don't report these disappearances, I'll be blamed for taking a hand in them."

Somehow, although I'd feared this, the moment still came as a shock. The Inquisitors. Witchcraft. I'd never been inside the Doge's palace—the Daylight Doge, not the Glass Doge—but they said the torture chamber was just a stairway away from the council chamber. They said the strappado meant tying your hands behind your back, hauling you to the ceiling and then dropping you from that height until the slack of the rope caught you, wrenching your arms from their sockets.

They said it was like the torments of Hell.

Gonzaga leaned back in the wooden chair. "I have...experience in not disappearing easily. Who were your last two applicants, anyway? An old pantaloon and a suckling babe."

"You think you can do better?"

A shrug. "I'm Cosimo Gonzaga."

Papa's mouth firmed. He didn't like foreigners. He particularly didn't like cocky foreigners. "I've never heard of such a person."

I had. And although he was far down my list of worries, I knew from our first meeting that he'd watch me drown in the canal sooner than risk his neck fishing me out again. My gut twisted. In ceding Benito to the Doge, had I doomed Lucia to a life of dependence on this man?

"I'm a condottiere formerly in the service of Sforza of Milan." Gonzaga paused momentarily. "We had a difference of opinion, and I found it wise to retire to Venice."

A mercenary. It was a respectable profession; Venice herself employed mercenaries to fight her wars. We were merchants and sailors, not knights or commanders. Most condottieres were honourable men who donated to Holy Church and performed their contracts faithfully. If they changed sides when their contracts ran out, well, that was just business.

I doubted Cosimo Gonzaga was an honourable man.

Papa glanced from the condottiere to Lucia and back again. "What interests you in an alliance with Caloprini?"

"It's time I married." Gonzaga spoke easily. "I need money to pay my debt to Sforza, and you need a man of the world to untangle your problems here." He cocked an eyebrow in our direction. "It's unlikely your daughters are killers or witches, but have you searched the house for bodies?"

Papa looked momentarily shocked, then intrigued. "There's nowhere they could have hidden them. Except in the canal. And then the bodies would have to be weighted."

"But we haven't killed anyone!" Filippa burst out, goaded into words. "Or done witchcraft!"

Papa's eyes narrowed. "Is there something you'd like to tell us, Filippa?"

He and Gonzaga waited expectantly. I looked at Filippa, willing her to keep silence. *No. No. No.*

She knew she was as guilty as me. "No," she said weakly. "It's nothing."

Gonzaga turned back to Papa. "As I said, signor, I don't believe my esteemed forerunners are dead. There's more to this than meets the eye. Leave it to me for a day or two, and I promise you won't have to call the Inquisitors."

Once again, Papa looked thoughtfully from Gonzaga

to Lucia and back again. Ordinarily, he'd be as reluctant to marry his daughter to a foreigner as he would to a glassmaker. But I knew what his decision would be. Anything to save him from scandal. "Signor, agreed. The house is yours. Act as you like. Just end this nightmare."

* * *

Papa rang for Maria and told us to wait in the portego. With the door of the study closed behind us, Filippa seized my arm.

"The Inquisitors," she choked. "Gemma, we have to tell them. If we make this one disappear, Papa will turn us over to them."

I put my hands to my head. "If we tell Gonzaga what we're up to, he'll marry Lucia. But I *know* him, Filippa. I've met him before. He's worse than Friuli. He's a killer."

Filippa paled. Mercifully, before she could ask another question, Maria joined us. There was nothing else to say. Lucia still hadn't spoken, her eyes blank and shadowed. I felt desperate. I had to fix this, but how?

When Papa and Gonzaga emerged from the study, Papa was more cheerful than he'd looked in days. He was even chuckling at something the condottiere said. "Get to know my daughters," he told Gonzaga. "I have business to attend to."

He went downstairs, and Gonzaga turned to us with a smile. "Will you show me to my room? I'd like to see where all these disappearances took place."

We stared at him woodenly until I realised that as the eldest, they were waiting for me to direct him. I moved reluctantly to the staircase. "Follow us."

Instead of falling into line, he snapped his fingers as if remembering something. "A moment. Your father neglected to tell me which of you is to be my bride."

On the first step, level with his eyes, I whipped around. "None of us!"

Gonzaga's eyebrows shot up—and he laughed.

There was an awkward silence. Then, to my surprise, Lucia spoke. "I'm Lucia, signor. I'm the youngest. I think I'm the one you mean."

The laughter left Gonzaga's face as he took my sister's hand. "Sweet lady. I am enchanted."

His voice was familiar. I could still hear it echoing between the narrow walls of a dark alley where I'd nearly been choked to death. *Kill her then. Do I seem to care?*

If I didn't know better, I might have been taken in. Luckily, Lucia wouldn't look him in the eye and pulled her hand away as soon as she could.

"Maria and I will show him upstairs." I spoke with decision. "You and Filippa have left your needlework on the loggia. You'd better get it before the rain starts."

Lucia shot me a grateful look. As the two of them retreated across the portego to the loggia, Gonzaga laughed. "You now, Signorina Gemma…" His voice dropped to a breath. "You I *could* see as a killer. You have just enough of the hellcat in you."

"You must meet a lot of women like that."

I put a sting into the words, but it apparently missed him. He said thoughtfully, "You're the first I've met with the wit to bargain her way out of a back-alley brawl."

My fingers tightened on the stair rail. "How did you know me?"

"Smell." He lifted an eyebrow. "The soap your laundress uses to wash your clothes. Lemon, cloves, and a hint of cinnamon and rosemary. That, combined with your voice and station."

I opened my mouth and closed it again. He smirked, clearly proud of his deductions.

"I see." I lowered my voice. "Then you'll understand that I'll be warning my sister about you, signor. Don't rely too much on flattery. We all know you're only interested in her dowry."

I turned and led the way upstairs to our sleeping-quarters. Gonzaga chuckled, but he didn't try to deprive me of my final word. Maria climbed in stolid silence on our heels. I threw the door open into the guest room.

"You'll sleep in here. You won't be the first." I pointed through the open communicating door. "That's our room. Papa will tell you he had a servant watching outside all night; we never left."

Gonzaga hooked his thumbs into his belt and then strolled into our room without permission. He turned, sparing a second casual glance for the mirror. Following him with Maria, I scrutinised his face for any sign of recognition.

But he turned from the mirror with apparent unconcern. "You were watched inside, too? I assume your chaperone was on guard. What did you see, donna?"

"Not *donna*. Just Maria," I snapped. Couldn't he see she was a Tartar?

"Donna Maria," he amended imperturbably. "What did you see?"

She slid a glance sideways at me. Conscious of Gonzaga's attention, I kept my face bland, but I willed her to remember the threat I'd made last night.

"Nothing," she said at last.

Gonzaga ran a thoughtful hand through his hair. "You were asleep?"

This morning, following my directions, she'd told Papa that she'd remained awake all night, but that the candle had burned out and when the sun rose, Benito had vanished. Now, her forehead creased as she tried to recall the false facts. Seeing this, Gonzaga lifted a hand.

"Let's have one thing clear, donna. I consider myself bound as if by the seal of confessional. Nothing you tell me will be repeated. You were asleep, weren't you?"

Maria glanced sidelong at me and spoke defensively: "I tried to keep awake, holy angels!"

"I make no reproach, donna. How can a woman who works hard all day keep her eyes open at night, anyway?"

Maria blinked in surprise.

Meanwhile, beads of sweat formed on my forehead. Maria hadn't told him I was forcing her to drink drugged wine, but five minutes with Gonzaga, even with me standing right here, and my control was slipping.

This man was dangerous.

"I'd like a private word with Signorina Gemma." Gonzaga led us back out into the portego and pointed toward the loggia that opened onto the canal front. "We'll talk on the balcony, by your leave."

He opened one of the glass doors and extended a hand to me. I didn't want a private conversation, but Signor Gonzaga was too much of a threat to leave to his own devices. I stepped through onto the balcony and let him close the door behind us, shutting us off from Maria's hearing, if not her sight.

He leaned against an arch, folding his arms with an indulgent smile. "You're still angry with me, aren't you?"

If I wasn't before, I would be today. "My sister's an innocent child," I snapped. "She'd be better off dead than married to someone like you."

"I see that you're a woman of the world, signorina." He was laughing at me. I didn't bother getting angrier.

"Why come here? If it's money you want, you should go somewhere else. Somewhere you won't…" I fumbled for the right word.

"Won't what?"

"Disappear. Like the others."

Over his shoulder, across the Grand Canal, I could

see the palazzo opposite ours. In the Daylight City, the Glass Doge's dwelling was derelict and abandoned, its feet swamped and mirrored in water.

Gonzaga lifted an amused eyebrow. "You're threatening me, signorina?"

"I'm warning you."

"I quake in my boots. No, I won't go elsewhere. Patricians as rich as your father don't often find themselves in such exquisitely difficult circumstances. This is the richest dowry in Venice at the moment, and it's open to just about anyone. I'd be a fool not to try it."

I didn't bother hiding my look of disgust. "I don't know why Papa let you inside the house. If it was me, I'd have thrown you out as soon as you said you were after the money."

A chuckle. "Why, what else should I marry for? Everyone marries for something. Money. Status. Appetite. That's the way the world works, and there's no need to be ashamed of it. Your father and I both benefit from this arrangement. He has a problem, and I can solve it for him. My problem is Sforza. He's angry that I switched sides before my contract expired, and because I chose unwisely, my men are dead and I'm on the run till I can repay what I owe."

"I'm amazed you're telling me this." I folded my arms. "Some marry for love."

"Well, this is a form of love, isn't it? Service? Exchange? Substitution?"

"It's profiteering."

"Signorina, I'm only answering your question. Why I'm here."

"Fine. Are we done?"

"No. I want you to tell me what *you* need." He'd been leaning on a pillar, but now he stood upright, pushing the hair from his face. "You and your sisters obviously know exactly what happened to Friuli and Mafei. But for some reason, you aren't telling. You're defying your father and risking the Inquisitors, and yet you remain firm. So, whatever the reason is, it's desperate enough to keep you silent. There's a secret that's oppressing you. Am I right?"

I stared at him, shocked that he understood. "Yes," I said before I could stop myself.

"Maybe there's something I can offer you. An alternative."

I swallowed. Filippa thought we could tell him. That he'd help us make up a plausible story. But we'd still be in debt to the Doge—and Gonzaga would marry Lucia.

I drew my mouth tight. "Oh. So you're willing to help me now that it's in your interest."

"I'm here to serve, signorina."

"You told them to kill me. Don't you remember? I was nearly *strangled* because of you." I yanked at the concealing ruff around my neck. "I've still got the bruises to prove it!"

From the moment I saw him in Papa's study yesterday,

93

I'd known what I planned for Cosimo Gonzaga. I'd been doubtful trading Friuli to the Glass Doge, and agonised ceding Benito. But trapping Gonzaga behind the glass, trading his life for *my* freedom, that would be a positive pleasure.

And then... For the first time I was able to glimpse a future. With our debt to the Doge paid, we could smash the mirror. No more dancing, true. And I would always know my house was haunted. But at least he would no longer have a hold over us. Future suitors, if they came, would see only the three of us sleeping soundly in our bed. With no solution for Papa, he'd have to forget the whole thing.

Maybe the Inquisitors would descend, but even Papa didn't want that. Threatening Maria had worked so far. Perhaps I could find some way to force Papa to be silent as well.

Gonzaga shrugged. "Believe me, I understand why you're angry. But I'm here to help, and frankly, I'm dead meat if I can't. Command me, signorina. Tell me how I can serve you."

You can serve yourself. Up, to the Glass Doge, on a plate. But of course I couldn't say that. I moved to the door, permitting myself a smile.

"Bad luck for you, signor. It's not in *my* interest to tell you a single thing."

I pushed open the glass door and stalked back into the portego, once more carrying off the honours of the final

94

word. Soon after, Gonzaga excused himself and went into the city on some matter of business.

I took the chance to find my sisters and tell them everything that he had done in the campo of Saint John and Saint Paul.

* * *

We did not see the condottiere again until dinner that evening. Whatever his errands were in the city, they'd involved having his beard trimmed and changing into a suit of new clothes, a sad grey-blue that well suited his olive complexion. Lightning-like lines of gold lace picked out the seams. In the dim candlelight, it was only at close quarters that you could see the coarseness of the weave and the straining lines across the back under the armscye that told of poor tailoring.

"The dye must have been cheap, too," I said with a sniff to Lucia as Maria lighted us upstairs. "It's an ugly blue and everyone wears it."

Filippa laughed. "You don't like him, I can tell."

We would have eaten our dinner in disgrace in our room if Gonzaga hadn't coaxed Papa into letting us attend the meal with the two of them. Amazingly, dinner was less awkward than I expected. Gonzaga kept the conversation going with tale after tale of his past exploits. He managed to draw even Lucia out of her shell with the story of how he won his gorgon-headed ring in a game of dice from a man who swore it would bring good luck.

"But it didn't bring him enough luck to win the game. So why do you wear it?" Filippa had asked.

Gonzaga, leaning back in his chair at the end of the meal, flicked a nut into the air and caught it in his mouth. "To keep anyone from learning the truth." He waggled an eyebrow at her.

"What truth?" Eyes wide, Lucia leaned forward.

"That I make my own luck."

All his stories were like that, I realised as we went upstairs. All of them revolved around his own cleverness, courage, and good taste.

"He talks about nothing but himself," I whispered. "And he treated me like a harlot the first time we met."

"He called you a killer and a hellcat." Lucia was a pale flutter of indignation next to me. "I heard him say it before you went upstairs this afternoon."

Her trust cut me. I was beginning to feel every inch a hellcat and worse than a killer. I was a betrayer of souls.

Before I could think of a response, Filippa whispered, "You're not, Gemma."

That was worse. Lucia believed I was a good person, but Filippa knew I wasn't. Filippa was complicit in what I'd done, and her words of comfort were meant for herself every bit as much as for me. I didn't know what was worse—the fact that I had corrupted her as quickly as I'd corrupted myself, or the fact that I'd made it easier by lying to her.

Maybe I was guilty, but I still had every reason to be angry. "What right does Gonzaga have to say things like that? How many men has he killed? How many harlots has he visited? The only reason he's in Venice at all is that he broke his contract and betrayed his duke."

"I don't want to marry him," Lucia confessed when we were in our room and Maria had gone to attend Mama.

Filippa looked determined. "You won't have to. Trust us."

It was only the thought of the Inquisitors that kept me from answering just as promptly. But after further thought, I nodded. "Gonzaga's a foreigner and a sellsword. No one will notice if he vanishes."

Maria returned from Mama's room while I was still crushing the laudanum into the wine. I didn't bother trying to hide what I was doing. When I was finished, Maria took the cup and stood looking at it for a little while.

"Something the matter?" I asked.

She shook her head wearily.

"Then drink." I watched until the cup was drained, then slipped into bed beside my sisters. Maria opened the door that communicated with the guest room, but it was empty. Gonzaga was still downstairs.

She returned slowly to the foot of our bed. "That one is not like the last two," she muttered. I got up on my elbows, realising that her drowsy words were directed to us. "You have forced me to drink, but what will he force you to do when I am asleep and cannot protect you?"

She felt her way to her chair and slumped into it. Still on my elbows, I stared into the dark with the skin crawling over spine and scalp. My sisters had heard Maria's words—Maria's curse—and they lay like the dead, neither breathing nor moving.

Ridiculous. I gave a soft snort of contempt and lay down. Gonzaga would never try anything; not with parents and servants within shouting-distance, not when it would put his dowry at risk. As for Maria, how little she knew of the forces that already violated my will. I was born to the patriciate of the Most Serene Republic. But because I was a woman, I might as well be a slave.

In the guest room, the door slammed open. Beside me, Lucia jumped. There was a burst of laughter—Papa's laughter—and then Gonzaga closed the door and shuffled into his room.

Lucia latched onto my elbow. *Don't be such a baby,* I wanted to scold her. But despite myself, I felt my pulse speeding up. In one respect, Maria was right. Gonzaga would be much more difficult to deal with than either Friuli or Benito.

But his next actions surprised me. His bed groaned as he collapsed onto it. He pulled off each boot with a dim grunt, snuffed his candle and pitched into the pillows. Within a few minutes he was breathing deeply and steadily.

"What's he doing?" Filippa's whisper was very soft and

rather nervous.

"I think he's asleep."

Lucia's grip on my arm relaxed.

"The fool," Filippa snickered. But I began to feel alarmed. Gonzaga had Papa eating out of his hand. Maybe he figured that with time, he wouldn't have to solve the mystery of our worn-out dancing shoes. A few more dinners, a few more late-night drinking sessions, the skilful deployment of all his charm—and who knew if Papa wouldn't go ahead and give him Lucia and the dowry and everything, purely for love?

Leaving me to deal with the Glass Doge on my own. Cunning of him, and the one course of action that I truly didn't know how to handle.

Presently, the mirror opened. As the three of us dressed, Gonzaga's heavy breathing continued, and I considered going into the guest room to wake him. But Maria's words prevented me. Knowing him, he'd get the wrong idea entirely.

I dawdled as I dressed, making as much noise as I dared, but the mercenary never shifted. Meanwhile, the Doge awaited our company, and I did not dare to keep him waiting. I nodded to my sisters, picked up the candle, and plunged through the cold glass.

We were halfway down the stairs when I heard a floorboard creak above.

Lucia gasped and grabbed my elbow, almost snuffing the candle. "What's that?"

We all held our breath. So did the man upstairs. The hard lump of anxiety in my gut unknotted.

Gonzaga was coming after all. Gonzaga was playing into my hands.

Voices carried well up and down this staircase. I didn't bother to whisper. "It's nothing, Lucia. Just a rat, I expect."

Fillippa snickered and nudged me with her elbow. "A *big* rat."

I lifted a finger to my lips.

He stayed far behind us all the way. We crossed the mirror-water, where the moonlight cast mazy patterns on the waves, without seeing or hearing from him. Inside the Doge's palazzo, we had already climbed the stairs before Gonzaga reached the door.

In the press and noise of the ballroom, Lucia lost her nervousness. She went up on tiptoe, craning her neck to see through the crowd. She was clearly looking for Benito, and I felt a twinge of worry—would he give away my secret? Would he tell her how thoroughly he had been trapped?

I didn't like letting her speak to him alone. I knew how tenuous was my control of this situation, how close I was to making one last slip that would doom us all. But it couldn't be helped; I had to speak to the Doge. I had to hope Benito did not yet fully comprehend his position.

Someone asked me to dance. I substituted Filippa in my place, and with both my sisters safely occupied, I searched the room for the Doge. Instead, I found Pollonia.

"Gemma," she greeted me. "Come onto the loggia, we're playing Capture the Hat."

A rowdy children's game did in fact seem to be going on in the loggia, though with tipsy adult players it better resembled a Tintoretto painting of Romans and Sabines. Join in such a game, me? I was a good girl.

I *had* been a good girl. Once.

"I can't, Pollonia. I have to find the Doge. I have another payment for him."

It happened without warning. One moment Pollonia stood in front of me laughing out of sparkling green eyes. The next moment the eyes were blank. No Pollonia behind them.

Her jaw moved awkwardly as if manipulated by a puppet's strings, and her expressionless voice said, "You wished to speak to me?"

I stared at her a moment before I understood. Then I backed away two steps, pressing a hand to my mouth. "Don't," I whispered. "Let go of her. Please."

"You said you came with another payment."

"Let me speak to you in your true form."

I jumped as a hand fell on my shoulder and the Doge spoke in my ear: "You would not care to see my true form."

Pollonia blinked and was herself again. Looking dazed, she pressed her hands to her temples and staggered away without speaking to either of us.

I turned to the Glass Doge, so terrified that it was

difficult to focus eyes or mind on him. "She's my friend," I whispered. "Please don't..."

One black eyebrow went up. "I am your friend, Gemma."

I hated being alone with him, but the last thing I needed was another of my sisters overhearing us. "I need to speak to you. In private."

He bowed and extended his arm. Cringing, I laid my fingertips on it, and we plunged through the nearest mirror. In the derelict ballroom on the other side, the air pressed lovingly close, a clinging winter damp. I shivered, but I was grateful for the wakefulness it brought.

Tonight. Just tonight, just long enough to pay my debt.

"I've brought my third payment," I told him, lacing my fingers together. "At least, he ought to have arrived by now. His name is Cosimo Gonzaga."

The Doge's eyes went out of focus for a moment. Then they found me again and smiled. "Indeed. He is here."

"You'll accept him as final payment?"

"On the usual terms. He must not return to the Daylight City before sunrise."

That would be the delicate part. "I'll need help. Pollonia distracted the last two, but I think Gonzaga may be harder to trick."

His unnaturally white teeth gleamed in the refracted candlelight. "It's your affair. You came here for freedom, didn't you?"

"Isn't it in your interest to help me?" Now I sounded

like Gonzaga, trying to make deals.

The Glass Doge curled his lip. "This is Daylight City talk. Service and exchange, substitution and sacrifice. There are no servants here, Gemma. Only the strong, the wilful, and the free."

"Free?" I looked through the glass at the dancers in the ballroom. "Then why can so many of these people never leave?"

"Because of *Venice*." The Doge almost spat the word. "This used to be my place, you understand. I *owned* Veneto. And then the men came and hemmed me in with their houses and churches, their bells and their bridges, until there was nowhere left for me but the backs of mirrors and the bottoms of wells and the abandoned houses where bitter old women dabbled in forbidden arts. Now this house is my prison. But I am not selfish. I would share it with the whole city, if I could."

I shivered.

"But I'll break out. They keep driving people here, these high lords of the Serene Republic. Jews. Nuns. Slaves. All the thousands of souls that dream of freedom and don't find it in the Daylight City, who come to me for the desire of their hearts. One day, there will be more lives here than there. The balance will tip, and the mirrors will open."

"I suppose I know how you feel," I said after a long, terrified moment. It was the only thing I could think of to say.

But I am not like the Doge. I could never be like the Doge.

He straightened a little, the tension rolling from his shoulders. "My time will come. Be sure your guest remains past dawn."

I nodded.

"And be sure you come back to dance with us tomorrow night."

I kept a tenuous grip on my panic. "Signor?"

"Your sister suggested smashing the mirror. It would be a shame to lose your company."

I laughed shakily. "Filippa's impulsive, that's all. Shouldn't we return? My sisters will be missing me." Sometimes, I forgot the Doge could hear everything we said in our house. Despite my words, my stomach knotted. What would happen if I defied him?

What would happen if I didn't?

* * *

With a whole night to endure before we could leave, I prowled the ballroom, refusing any offer to dance. I was sick of this, I realised. Sick of the same music, the same dances, the same partners who sometimes pulled me too close or let their hands linger in unwelcome places. Freedom, the Doge had said. But it didn't feel like freedom when I had to push strangers away to arm's length, any more than it felt like freedom locked away in a convent or palazzo.

I looked on the loggia, but the rowdy games had finished and I eventually unearthed Pollonia chattering with one of the men in an alcove. I blundered between them, calling Pollonia's name, before I registered the grey-blue suit with gold lace.

Gonzaga.

But he didn't bother me. He bowed and excused himself, and I was left with Pollonia.

"You know him?" she observed with a smile. "He was asking about Benito and your sister."

"Of course he was. Wretch!"

"Another suitor? He seemed jealous."

I'd told Pollonia about Papa's ultimatum. Now, I sank my mask into my hands and shook my head. "Pollonia, he's awful."

"We can deal with him. Just like the others."

I looked at her gratefully. "We'll have to be cunning."

"There are ways to keep a man from using his mind at all." Pollonia lips twitched. "Leave it to me."

I knew nothing of such arts, but I had to be grateful she was employing them on my behalf. "You're a true friend," I began. And then stopped myself. I couldn't say goodbye or tell her I'd miss her. The Doge would hear and know.

"Are you happy here?" I questioned, forgetting that I had already asked.

Pollonia's eyes behind the mask were shuttered and wary, though I knew it wasn't me she was afraid of. "It's better than the Daylight City," she said at last.

"Oh?"

She hitched a shoulder. "In the Daylight City I lived at the beck and call of others. Beaten and upbraided if I didn't please. It's different here."

"No Inquisitors," I agreed. For a moment, I was tempted. As frightened as I was of the Glass Doge, the Inquisitors and their torments frightened me more. If I kept the mirror open, I would always have an escape.

But how much of mind and soul would I have to give up? I looked sidelong at Pollonia. "Before, when you went away and the Doge—"

She didn't say a word. Just put a warning hand on my wrist. Chills ran up my arm at her touch, lifting the hair on my head. For a moment, we waited for the Doge to materialise.

But he didn't, and at last Pollonia let go. "It's the price I have to pay," she said.

"I thought there were no bargains here."

"Oh, but there are. They're just all bad ones."

"I don't want any bargains," I said wearily. "I want to be myself. The way a cloud in the sky is herself, or a swallow in the rafters. To change when I will. To go when I will."

"If you know of a way to become a cloud or a swallow, tell me by all means." Pollonia's voice was laden with sarcasm. "In the meantime, at least this existence was *my* choice. Most women don't even get so much."

I felt sorry for her. But I had no way to say it.

The hours passed. I didn't speak to Gonzaga, and to my

106

surprise, I didn't see him speaking to Lucia either. Instead, he worked his way around the whole room, chatting and bowing for all the world like a merchant sniffing out lucrative connections at a party.

I left it as long as I dared before starting back to the Daylight City. As I prepared to leave, Pollonia came to me once more, touching my shoulder and only winking. From there, she worked her way across the crowded room in Gonzaga's direction.

Sunrise was nearly on us. I only had to catch Lucia and Filippa's eyes across the room and make a slight motion of the head. Neither of them were slow in responding. I met them on the steps and led them to the doorway with my heart thumping, sure that Gonzaga must have seen us leave.

Outside, the light was bright, diffused through the morning fog. A hand closed on my heart. Was I too late? In my desperation to trap Gonzaga, had I trapped all of us by mistake?

"Hurry," I whispered to my gondolier.

On our side of the canal, I broke into a run. No sound of pursuit made it past our own slamming feet and laboured breath. Up the staircase, onto the piano terzo and across the bare floorboards into the reflection of our room. The mirror yawned before us, and thank Heaven, through it could be seen the dim outlines of our bed and even Maria, a dark blur in the chair beyond.

I caught my sisters by the hand and yanked them

through the frame.

As we staggered to a halt on the other side, Filippa gave a muffled giggle of relief. I shushed her with a lifted hand and listened.

Nothing.

The mirror remained open. Did we cross too soon, after all? For a moment I prayed for it to close as eagerly as I'd prayed for it to remain open as I ran up the stairs.

A network of reflected gold began to play on the ceiling.

The mirror closed.

I leaned my forehead against the glass, tears stinging my eyes. At last. It was over, it was done. We were free of the Glass Doge.

Filippa caught my arm, put her lips to my ear. "Smash it!"

My skin prickled. Would the Doge hear? What could I say? "Don't be foolish! If we break the glass now, we'll wake Maria, and they'll guess where we've been."

Filippa looked doubtful.

I was doubtful myself. What could the Doge could do to me if I disobeyed him and stayed home tonight? Or worse, if I smashed the mirror? Maybe it was wisest just to do as he said.

"Just leave it for now, Filippa," I whispered. "If Benito knew about the mirrors, you can bet the Inquisitors do too."

Reluctantly, Filippa nodded. Maria shifted in her chair, her breath catching, but didn't wake. Hastily, the three of us stripped off our finery and crawled into bed. I heaved a sigh and snuggled under the bedclothes, letting the worry drain out of me. At least Gonzaga was no longer a threat to Lucia and the Doge no longer had a claim on us. For the first time in days, I felt I could really sleep.

I was hovering on the edge of unconsciousness when slow footsteps passed in the portego outside. Then the door to the guest room opened and the sound of boots echoed across the marble floor.

Someone yawned.

I bolted upright and yanked the bed-curtains back. Cosimo Gonzaga stood in the next room plucking at the latches of his jacket. When he heard the curtain-rings rattle, he turned and saw me. Turned and smiled and bowed, ironically low.

* * *

"What are we going to *do?*" Lucia was close to tears. "I won't marry him! Papa can't make me do it!"

I was surprised. I didn't know she had it in her.

"I wish it had been Benito. I wish I hadn't left him there, Gemma!"

Gonzaga was meeting with Papa even now. The breakfast tray had come up, and I'd torn open the loaf of white bread in an attempt to eat something, but now I shoved it away. "Oh, Lucia, for heaven's sake, what good is wishing? Be quiet and let me think!"

Her lip wobbled, but she didn't speak again. I was instantly sorry for the words, but she didn't know what was at stake for me. Once Lucia married Gonzaga, Filippa and I would be packed off to the convent again. I'd be separated from the mirror, unable to pay that final price to the Doge.

I didn't want to think about what might happen after.

"What if Papa calls the Inquisitors?" Even Filippa had her arms around herself like a child trying to seek comfort.

I swallowed. "Gonzaga wants his dowry. He won't let the Inquisitors anywhere near Lucia."

"That doesn't help the rest of us. What are we going to say to Papa?"

"To Papa? Nothing. Tell him Gonzaga is lying."

"He won't believe us."

"It's the only way. We mustn't confess to anything, understand? If we confess, we're dead."

A knock sounded on the door, making us all jump. I got to my feet, trying to calm myself. I wouldn't go down without a fight. Not even now that Papa knew everything.

"Come in," I called.

Maria entered. "Signor Gonzaga."

Not Papa? I'd expected him to come storming up in a white rage.

"Bring him in," I said faintly.

Gonzaga entered. No Papa. No apparent sign that he was about to drag Lucia to the altar. In fact, he was no longer wearing his suit of blue-grey; he'd changed back into the shabby clothes he'd worn when he first came to the palazzo.

He doffed his bonnet and bowed. "Good morning, signorinas. I wonder if I might sit with you a while?"

We did not move or speak as he settled himself into a chair and crossed ankle over knee. Or as he smiled serenely at Lucia. "You're looking radiant this morning, signorina. As ever."

She swallowed convulsively.

"You must have slept well." Amusement laced his voice.

I slammed my hands onto the table and exploded. "Signor! A private word, if you please."

With a smirk, he got up and followed me through the portego and onto the loggia, where I turned on him in something like desperation.

"What is this?" If a whisper could be shrill, mine was. "I know you followed us last night. I know you've been to see Papa. For the love of heaven, tell me what is happening."

He lifted both hands with a laugh. "Calm down. Nothing is happening."

I gasped for breath, trying to formulate the right question. "What did you tell him?"

"I didn't tell your father anything."

Could I believe him? He smiled at me encouragingly. My fear receded, leaving me anxious and disoriented. "Nothing? Why not?"

"I didn't think it would be in my interests. Not just yet."

"Do you ever think of anyone's interests but your own?"

"Frequently. You'd be surprised how often other people's interests coincide with one's own. A man can go a long way serving others." He jerked his head toward the glass doors; Maria, Filippa, and Lucia stood within, pretending not to stare at us. "Shall we?"

"No! What interests are you talking about?"

He laughed silently. "Not so fast. If you remember, I asked you a similar question yesterday, and you didn't answer me. Let's trade, shall we? You tell me what you want, and I'll tell you what I want."

What did I want? The freedom to live my life the way I wanted it. To protect my sisters from the Inquisition, the convent, or a bad marriage. And Gonzaga locked safely away beyond the glass.

He read the stubbornness in my face and nodded toward the portego. "Should I ask your sisters instead?"

I clenched my fists. I had to keep control of this situation. "Over my dead body! If you've got something to ask them, you'll ask in my presence or not at all."

He tipped his head to one side, lifting an eyebrow, as if considering it. Then he nodded. "That sounds fair. You won't prevent me speaking to them in your presence, and I won't try to get information from them in your absence. It's a deal."

Trapped!

"No deal," I protested. "I'm telling you that neither of

them wants to speak to you, you hear me?"

"No doubt you've convinced them that I'm a scoundrel of the blackest dye."

"If the name fits you, signor, you can't complain."

"A hit!" He laughed, more proud than sorry. Then: "You're just like your father, you know."

I was stupefied. *"What? I am nothing like—"*

"Trying to control everything. And the worse things get, the tighter you clench your fists. Lady Gemma. Empress Gemma. How long has it been since your sisters dared to have a single thought you didn't personally put into their heads?"

My fists had been clenched. At his words, they popped open. When he finished speaking, I slapped him.

Or tried to. He caught my wrist. I gritted my teeth and pulled, but he kept his grip.

He was much stronger than me, and for one moment it all bubbled up into my mind, the panic I'd felt strangling to death in the alley...

I whimpered, and he let me go. "I'm the only one who cares for them," I said, dangerously close to tears. "I'm the only one trying to protect them."

Gonzaga swallowed and lowered his voice, although his words were no less relentless. "You need to stop trying. By this point, you're the one they need protection from. Let them learn to protect themselves."

There was truth in his words. I was the one who took them through the mirror in the first place. And after my efforts to fix things, they'd be lucky not to burn as witches.

But even if I'd been foolish, I wasn't the one actually threatening to turn them over to the Inquisitors or force them into an unwanted marriage.

"Are you trying to cozen me?" I said. "Do you think you're better than me, Cosimo Gonzaga? Try pointing the finger at yourself. You forced me to accompany you that night. You got me unmasked and nearly killed. If it wasn't for you, none of this would have happened."

For a moment I thought I'd quenched him. Then he gave a soft huff of laughter. "Tell yourself that, signorina. But don't forget I offered you a deal. I'll speak to your sisters in your presence, or I'll speak to them out of it. You choose."

There was really no way I could prevent him speaking to my sisters in private. I had no other choice. "Fine. In my presence, if you please."

"It's a deal." He held out his hand and reluctantly, I shook it.

"One more thing." I touched the tip of my tongue to my lips, trying to appear unconcerned. "How did you get back to the Daylight City this morning?"

He smirked. "Oh, Gemma, Gemma. That's not part of the deal."

"But it's for sale." I gave half a twisted smile. "Is there anything you have that isn't?"

He chuckled and shook his head. "Oh ho ho, you are a

fierce one."

I followed him back into the portego, infuriated but not defeated. He'd patronised me. He'd tried to drive bargains with me. But he hadn't told Papa our secret.

He'd given us another chance. And tonight, I promised myself, tonight he'd stay beyond the glass. Somehow, I'd make sure of it.

* * *

"You've returned." The Glass Doge was almost smug. "I am overwhelmed."

My cheeks warmed, but fear kept my pride in check. I checked that my sisters were not within earshot before muttering, "I don't know how it happened, but Gonzaga escaped somehow. It wasn't through our mirror."

A tilted black eyebrow. "I see."

For a moment I wondered if the Doge himself had helped Gonzaga escape. A second thought banished the idea. I could suspect the Doge of quite a lot, but letting anyone escape his web was not one of those things.

"How did he do it, your serenity? You must know."

"Who is it that tells me what I must or must not know?" I didn't mistake his dreamy mood for carelessness. "I have forgotten a great many things through the ages. And it makes no difference to me how I collect my debts."

My heart was a lump of ice. "But we had a bargain. You accepted him. It's not my fault he escaped."

The Doge's gaze pinned me down. "What, signorina? Do you debate stipulations and matters of contract with me? Shall two of us play at that game? Do not begin a dish you have not the stomach to finish!"

I pressed my lips together.

"Wise child." He showed his eerie white teeth.

"So what happens now? You give Gonzaga the same choice you gave me?" I imagined what the condottiere might do in order to meet the Doge's terms, and shuddered.

"Perhaps."

Somehow I had to get him on my side. *Think, Gemma.* Even the Doge wants something. Even the Doge is willing to make bargains. Lives. He wanted enough lives to open the glass, and I was valuable to him because I brought him captives. "I should warn you." I began lightly. "Gonzaga plans to tell my father about the city beyond the glass. If you don't keep him here past dawn, he'll tell Papa, and Papa will confiscate the mirror, maybe even destroy it. You gave me a year and a day to finish paying my debt, but unless you can keep Gonzaga past dawn, I may not have the rest of the year. I may only have days, and you will lose him and me both."

I curtseyed, but the Doge lifted a finger. "Wait."

My heart lifted. I'd bring him to terms yet. "Your serenity?"

"A year and a day, you say? No, I'm afraid that's no longer the period of the contract."

116

I stared.

"As you said, we had a bargain. You promised me this soul and did not follow through on it. The terms, signorina, are three days."

"Three *days?*" I yelped.

"Which means you have until tomorrow night to pay me the man you promised."

Tomorrow night.

I gulped for air, but the warmth of the ballroom almost choked me. And then, when I thought nothing could be worse, worse came.

"And if you fail," the Doge said, "I take your sister in payment. Enjoy the evening, signorina."

"No, wait!" I lunged after him and grabbed his sleeve in both hands, forcing him to face me again. "My sister? What do you mean? I'm the only one still to be paid for!"

He came around with a gloating smile. "On the contrary, my dear. You have already paid for yourself. Signorina Filippa still remains to be redeemed."

"No." I swallowed. "No, no, no, no. I paid Benito for Filippa. I *paid* for Filippa."

"Pardon me! You never specified who the payment was for. In that case, it was applied to yourself. You have until tomorrow night, signorina."

He pulled at his cuff, but I didn't let go. Desperation gave me strength. *"No.* You *have* to help me. You have to promise you won't let him escape, for the love of God!"

His free hand caught me across the face, catching me

off-guard. I recoiled with a yelp of astonishment. Even wearing a mask, the blow stung.

The Doge was livid, his eyes huge and blazing, the hand he'd struck me with trembling like a leaf in the wind. There was a deadly silence. Almost every single person in the room had stopped speaking or dancing at once and now stood gazing at me with murder in their eyes.

What did I say? What nerve did I strike?

With a deep breath, the Glass Doge lifted both hands to his head, smoothing back his iron-grey hair. The motion seemed to break some spell and the denizens of his palazzo returned to their conversations, blunting the silence with the buzz of their words.

The colour returned to his cheeks; a little sanity to his eyes. "I have told you before, signorina. This is not the Daylight City. You must fend for yourself."

He bowed perfunctorily and strode away. As ever, the crowd parted like water to let him pass. In the same moment, Cosimo Gonzaga materialised by my side. "Gemma! What's all this about? Did he hurt you?"

I had my hand pressed to my smarting cheek, and he reached up to move it aside so he could see. I yanked away from him in a passion of fear and indignation. "Don't touch me, *dog!*"

I wanted him to leave, but he just stood next to me and folded his arms while I kneaded my cheek and prodded the cut on the inside of my lip.

"Let me take you home," he said presently.

Go home? Lose my chance to trap him here? Panic gripped me, and I straightened. "No! It's not time to go home yet."

He looked skeptical.

I tasted salt and iron in my mouth, but I lifted my chin. "It's fine. I want to stay. Let's dance."

The cynical twist came back to the corner of his mouth. "I see," he said, and then, "By all means."

Taking my hand, he led me to the centre of the floor. The dance was the pavane, a lugubrious peregrination of drums and flutes that I had never liked; I preferred the livelier galliard or saltarello.

It would be a long time till dawn.

Gonzaga took my hand, and we began our slow promenade down the centre of the room. For a moment he didn't speak, but I sensed the words building up in him till he leaned down and said under the sound of drums: "This place stinks of witchcraft."

"Don't," I said sharply. I'd never said the word aloud. I didn't want to think what the Glass Doge would do if he heard it.

Gonzaga saw my nervousness and a little understanding came into his eyes. He nodded ahead of us several places in the set. "Who is the masked youth dancing with Lucia? Is that Mafei?"

Benito. "The last suitor," I said bitterly. "You know of him?"

"I do." He was silent for a while, watching them as

we moved through the dance. I knew the reason for his interest in them, and found that I was gritting my teeth. All day, I'd had to sit meekly while Gonzaga did his best to charm Lucia. I'd silently fumed while he told stories and jokes and even drew her out to talk about herself. I'd never seen anything like it. No, but I had. I'd watched the canal brats sit on the doorstep of the empty palazzo across from ours, playing a fish on a hook. Pull and slack, pull and slack, till before the poor fish knew what happened, it was lying on the doorstep with a knife in its gut.

"I was wrong." I bit the words off angrily.

Gonzaga turned his attention to me.

"Benito would have been perfect for Lucia. I ought to have let her have him."

Gonzaga shook his head wearily. "One of these days, I'll wake up and it will suddenly occur to me. Aha! Signorina Gemma *doesn't like me!* And it will all make sense."

I returned to my silent rage.

"And the other suitor? The first one?"

"Over in the corner, with the cup of wine and the blonde," I circled him slowly, my clammy fingers barely touching his. "The greybeard."

Gonzaga clicked his tongue. "Now I'm hurt, signorina. You made it clear that *I* was the worst thing that ever dragged its lousy carcass in your door. I assumed the rest were a sort of cross between Adonis and Sir Galahad."

"It wouldn't have mattered if they were. Lucia won't be forced to marry anyone she doesn't like."

"And who would make her?" Gonzaga snorted. "She's a reasonable girl; she'll see sense... Tell me, signorina. Why did you begin to come here?"

It was his turn to circle me. I resisted the urge to turn with him, to keep an eye on him. "When the mirror is open, it looks different. The glass fogs over, and sometimes cool air blows in... I smelled it one night, the city beyond the glass. Sweet and earthy."

"Like rain?"

"Like rot. When I touched the glass, my hand went through. Filippa and Lucia were frightened, but I wanted to find out where it led. I was sick of being shut up all the time. So we ventured through—and we followed the sound of music here."

And I'd regretted it ever since. And I was going to lose Filippa because of it.

"You wanted to dance?"

"Ciel, no! I've had dancing-lessons all my life. Even in the convent, because it was known some of us would leave to marry. No. I wanted to be *free*."

The music stopped, the dance ending. Gonzaga looked at me with the same calculating look that had been in his eyes when he stared at Lucia. At once, I came back on my guard.

He only said, "Free. What do you mean by that?"

No one had ever bothered to ask before, and so for a moment I didn't know what to say. "I don't want to be told what to do anymore. Not by Papa. Not by a husband."

Not by the Doge. "Not by anyone. I want to be who I was meant to be. I want to matter. I want to do what I want and go where I want."

The cynical twist in the corner of his mouth deepened as he looked at me.

I lifted my chin. "You don't expect to hear such things from a woman?"

He didn't laugh. He became deadly serious. "No. I would expect to hear something of the sort from most women of your station. Born men, they would be accustomed to command and govern the world. You especially." He nodded toward me. "I flatter myself I have your father's measure pretty accurately by now. He worries that any deviation from the expectations of those around him will harm him. He forces his daughters to behave exactly as he believes will make himself, and them, look best to others. And the less conformable the events happening in his household, the more he tightens his grip. Oh, I'm not surprised to see you kicking against the goads, Gemma."

"Then why do you make faces at me?"

"Do you really think that a man's life is much different?"

"You must be joking. I cannot even leave my *house* without a donna…"

"Courtesans leave their houses without chaperones. Do you think they are free? Running to the beck and call of the Zuan Friulis of the world? Beaten and upbraided if they refuse?"

122

I felt my cheeks heat. "How dare you compare—"

He interrupted. "Look at young Mafei, there. As a glassmaker, he can never set foot outside the lagoon. He may have been born male, but not only will he never travel, he'll also legally be a minor in his father's house, little better than a servant, until the day he's emancipated by deed or by death."

"He *is* emancipated."

"Then he's better off than any other man his age in Venice. Or look at your father. Perhaps you think your father is free. Each transaction in his warehouse is taxed, and the whole business depends on the goodwill of manufacturers, shipmasters, and the Grand Council itself, to the extent that when I entered his house, he was about to report the three of you to the Inquisitors just to save his own neck. Does *that* seem like the action of a free man?"

"Papa lets himself be frightened," I said contemptuously.

"Better men than he have fallen into that bondage. Or perhaps you think I am free. I considered myself free of a contract once. I misjudged. And now I am trying to save my life in Venice by flattery of a girl half my age. Does that seem to you like freedom?"

"You said yourself that my father has a harsh grip. What's wrong with wanting more freedom than I have?"

"Nothing at all. Just be sure you actually understand what freedom is. What *you* dream of doesn't exist." He jerked a thumb at his chest. "The best freedom I've found in a life much longer and more active than yours, is the kind that comes when people love you so much that they'll lay themselves down to give you what you want. And there's only one way to get that kind of love. You find out what *they* need, and you give it to them."

He straightened. "You ought to try it sometime, Gemma, instead of demanding that the world give you what you want for nothing. They might quickly find that you *do* matter, very much." He glanced across the room to where Lucia and Benito stood with their heads bent together, talking. "Now if you'll excuse me, the question I find most fascinating at the present is not what you need, but what your sister needs."

He pushed through the crowd toward Lucia and Benito. I watched him go bleakly. His words were all very well, maybe they even sounded noble, but I knew they only went so far. To save us, to give us what we truly needed, Gonzaga must yield himself to the Doge tonight. He must pay Filippa's debt for her and relieve Lucia of his attentions. He must give up his freedom forever, maybe even his very soul.

But he never would, because there was nothing in it for him.

No one would. And that was where his reasoning broke down. I could never work hard enough to earn a sacrifice like that. I could only use force or trickery. I *had* to use them, or I'd lose Filippa, and Papa really *would* call the

Inquisitors.

The only person who might possibly be convinced to help me was Pollonia. I began to search the room for her, but I didn't get far before Benito loomed up in front of me. "Signorina Gemma," he said.

Plague! I fell back a step, swallowing. Till now, I'd successfully avoided my victims.

"Benito." My conscience was a wreck. I couldn't look him in the eye. "Where—where's Lucia?"

"She's speaking to the mercenary." Benito sighed. "He might as well have his chance at her. I never will."

I closed my eyes, sensing the pain that lay behind his words. "Benito... I'm sorry. I'm so, so sorry. Please believe me."

"It's a little late for that."

Both of us were masked, but I'd never felt so exposed. "Does she know you can never leave?"

"I can't tell her." A silence. "I've tried."

"Oh, *ciel,*" I whispered. I was only beginning to realise what a tight control the Doge kept of everyone in his palazzo.

"At least," Benito's voice fell just as low, "at least I get to see her."

He bowed slightly and left. Uselessly, I clenched and unclenched my hands. Everything I'd done was wrong. I was trapped in this every bit as much as he was. And there was no way out but forward.

I couldn't save Benito, but maybe I could still save

Filippa.

I spotted Pollonia at last among the musical instruments. The musicians had taken a rest, and she was seated at the spinet, rattling out a galliard. Admirers surrounded her like the wandering stars. I slipped into the midst of them, and she looked up at me and winked, then kept playing.

When the musicians returned and the admirers dispersed, Pollonia came to me. "Gemma—what foul luck we've had, my dear!"

I lowered my voice to a whisper. "What happened last night? How did Gonzaga escape?"

The smile left her eyes. Pollonia shook her head, serious for once. "Let it go, Gemma. I can't help you any more."

I seized her arm. "I'm going to lose my *sister*, Pollonia."

"And if I do anything to help you, I'll run afoul of the one you know of." She pulled away from me.

I could think of nothing to threaten her with or force her hand. I didn't know her well enough to know what she feared, except the Doge. And although I had threatened and cajoled both Maria and my sisters, somehow I couldn't, I just couldn't use the Doge to threaten one who was already in his power.

I pulled her closer, whispering into her ear. "There must be something you want. Something I can do for you. Anything."

For a moment I thought the Doge was lurking at the

126

back of her eyes, they were so dead and despairing. "There's nothing you can do for me, Gemma."

"There is. I can tell." She wouldn't look at me like that if there was nothing she wanted. "Everyone wants something."

Pollonia grimaced, and I realised she was fighting back tears. Her voice was the merest thread of a whisper. "If you want to do something for me, free me from this place."

I let go of her arm, my hopes sinking.

She dragged in a sniff. "But that's impossible, isn't it?" Her voice was satirical, as if she was blaming me, and I didn't know why.

"I can't help that, can I?" Now I was the one close to tears.

"Apparently not." Pollonia brushed past me.

I felt as if I couldn't breathe. I elbowed my way through the dancers and out onto the loggia. There, hidden by an angle of the wall, I slid down, curled my arms around my knees and shivered. The sky was already grey in the east, and I realised I was dreading the dawn.

Chapter 4.

When we reached home, my sisters crept into bed and fell asleep. I didn't bother to join them. Instead, I dressed in a day gown and sat down to my needlework. But stitching only allowed me to focus on my troubles.

What would I tell Filippa? How would I tell her that the burden I'd forced onto her conscience had not been for her sake at all—it was for mine?

If only Gonzaga would not return this morning. If *only* he would just stay beyond the glass—

The door to his room opened, and my heart fell.

He yawned and sat on the bed to pull off his boots. Either the Doge couldn't hold him, or wouldn't. Either there was some excellent reason for the Doge to let him go, or he had a way to escape.

Before I knew what I was doing, I was standing in the doorway between our rooms.

A gold candlestick lay on the coverlet next to him. When Gonzaga heard my feet, he casually draped his jacket over it and stood up, stifling a second yawn behind his hand. "Something I can do for you, signorina?"

I'd seen a hundred of the same candlesticks in the palazzo beyond the glass. Gonzaga might believe in earning his way, but he evidently wasn't above pilfering himself some gratuities. "You're always so obliging, Signor Lightfingers."

His face didn't change. "You talk as if that's a bad thing."

I couldn't give in to the temptation to bandy words with him. "I have to speak to you. Will you meet me on the loggia after breakfast?"

"Of course."

I closed the door and retreated to my needlework. The sun rose high. Maria got up and locked the communicating door, then went out to begin her day's work. I stitched on, barely seeing my work, worrying about tonight. How would I predict what might happen? I was not good at planning. Something would go wrong. I would fall to pieces. I would lose Filippa.

It was a relief when the time came and Gonzaga met me on the loggia.

He found me sitting in a corner of the long balcony, still trying to marshal my thoughts. It was a pale, cold day at the end of winter and a faint mist hung over the city, softening the light, bluing the spires and domes, and muting the voices of those passing in the canal.

Gonzaga looked down at me with a wry twist in his mouth and said, "Where's the faithful Maria? I'm surprised at you, signorina. What would Papa say?"

"I'm past caring what Papa says." I held out a purse. "I want to buy something from you, signor."

He weighed the bag in his hands and laughed. "What, Gemma? Willing to drive a bargain at last? What's in here?"

"All my jewels. I don't have much money but that's in there as well. It ought to be worth something, and it's all I have."

"Then let's hear what I'm to give you in exchange."

"I need to know how you return from the city beyond the glass."

Gonzaga gave another soft laugh. The purse dropped into my lap.

"Oh ho, that's your game, is it, my Delilah? 'Tell me wherein thy great strength liest.' I think not."

I narrowed my eyes. "But you said it was for sale. So if this isn't enough to buy it, what is?"

He crossed his arms. "I asked you for information two days ago. You refused to give me a word. Since then, I've had to discover most of what I need to know with great care, and at great risk to myself. No, signorina, I don't think there's anything you can do for me now."

An awful possibility struck my mind. "You told Papa about the Doge?"

He cocked his head. "No," he said after an agonisingly long time. "No, because I don't yet have what I need." He must have seen the anxiety on my face, because he added, "Don't fear! I won't tell him anything without letting you know first."

Of course, there was no reason to worry about Papa learning our secret now. If I couldn't save Filippa, nothing mattered.

My face must have betrayed my despair, because Gonzaga stepped closer, bending to look into my eyes. "Gemma?"

I tried to speak, but when I opened my mouth, to my horror, a sob escaped. I jumped up and tried to pass him, but he stepped in front of me, catching my hands in both his.

His voice was more gentle and caring than I'd ever heard from a man before. "What is it, Gemma? You can tell me, you know."

I hiccupped another sob and burst into tears. Gonzaga stiffened for a moment. Then he put his arms somewhat gingerly around my shoulders and drew me against him, shushing me like a frightened animal. Scorn, jeers, or even blows I could have resisted and returned with interest, but his gentle touch broke down every defense, every suspicion. For that moment, I forgot all my dislike and distrust of the man. I forgot who he was and what I was trying to do to him. He was not Gonzaga any more; he was only comfort.

I hid my face in his chest and sobbed until there was a damp patch on the cheap broadcloth where he'd pressed my head. And far away, like a voice from a childhood that never was, he said:

"Tell me, Gemma. Tell me what's wrong."

"It's the Doge," I hiccuped, when I could speak. "He said that we have to st-tay unless we can make someone else stay instead."

"Plague!" He grabbed my shoulders and set me back from him. To the space that opened, there returned in a flood the suspicion and distrust that had always been between us. "Gemma, look at me. Is that what happened to Friuli and Mafei?"

My mind was beginning to work again. I swallowed and nodded. "I only did it for Filippa and Lucia. You don't know what the Doge is like. He sees everything. He hears everything." I shuddered. I wasn't acting. "Even in this house, he watches us through the mirrors. He's probably listening to us now."

A soft intake of breath. "And I was to be third. Is that right?"

I bought time by fishing in my pocket for a handkerchief and wiping my nose. "Someone has to be," I said cautiously. "And soon. If we don't make the final payment tonight..."

I gulped air.

"Tonight," he prompted, his eyes wary.

"If we don't make the final payment tonight, then he'll keep her forever."

His hands tightened on my shoulders. "Her? Who?"

She was my only trump card. "Lucia," I lied.

Gonzaga let go of me.

For a little while, he paced to and fro on the loggia, rubbing his chin with a thoughtful hand. I sat down and, because it could not possibly hurt, I went on sniffling into my handkerchief at intervals. Gonzaga turned. "When did you learn this?"

"Last night."

A flicker of humour quirked his mouth. "And you told him what you thought of it? And he struck you. Now I understand." He went back to his pacing. After a moment he said, "It will have to be another substitute, that's all. Venice is full of canal brats and beggars. Leave it to me."

"Oh, we can't do *that*."

He wheeled around. "Why not? You've played this game ruthlessly enough till now, signorina. Haven't you the stomach to play it to the end?"

My cheeks coloured. Perhaps I should be concerned for some poor child he was proposing to hand over to the Doge, but that didn't prompt my objection. "It's not *my* stomach you should worry about. I've had enough trouble getting my sisters to stand by while I trade their suitors to the Doge. I don't know what they would do if they saw me play the same trick on an orphan child."

He saw the force of that, but drummed his fingers against his elbow impatiently. "It will need to be *someone*."

"Will it?" I resisted the urge to touch my tongue to my lips. "Couldn't she simply escape him?"

"Escape him?" Gonzaga frowned. "How?"

The tears swimming in my eyes were genuine. So was

the defeated tone of my voice. "That's all I wanted you to tell me. You know how to get out of there. You must have some...key."

He looked at me, his face briefly shuttered. Then he gave a soft laugh and spread his hands wide. "I've nothing of the kind. No, I got out using the mirrors in the Doge's ballroom. They lead straight into the Daylight City." He pointed to the empty and ruined palazzo opposite ours. "It's not difficult."

The mirrors in the ballroom. The mirrors I went through when I spoke to the Doge in private.

Of course. Why hadn't I thought of them myself?

I swallowed. "But they don't open for just anyone. When I touch them, they're solid."

"Not for me."

A lump crawled up my throat. "Oh ciel. Then what about my sister?"

Gonzaga tugged on his chin. "Leave it to me. I'll speak to the Doge. I'll find someone to trade. Don't worry about Lucia." He flashed a smile at me. "I won't let her go without a fight. She's much too important to my future."

He patted my cheek in a fatherly way and left. At first I was reassured. Gonzaga would certainly come up with something. But he didn't know that the real person in danger was Filippa, not Lucia. What would he do when he found out?

I buried my head in my hands. I couldn't afford to trust Gonzaga. I needed my own solution. If only I could open and close the mirrors in the Doge's palazzo…

Pollonia must know. But she was too afraid to tell me. The Doge knew, but he never would. And Gonzaga pretended not to.

Think, Gemma, think…

There had to be a way through the mirrors. They opened for him, but not for me. They opened for the Doge, but not for me.

Was the Doge controlling them? Did the Doge open and close the mirrors for Gonzaga? And why? If it was perverse pleasure he wanted, why single us out and not Gonzaga?

I closed my eyes, touching my cheek where the Doge hit me not so many hours previously. It was still tender and across my cheekbone there was a bruise where one of his rings had caught me. In my mind's eye, I saw him lifting both his hands to smooth back his hair—long white slender hands like a woman's, with immaculate nails.

He'd never strike Gonzaga that way. Gonzaga had led a rough life; he wouldn't react with the same pain and shock as I did. Was that what drew the Doge to us? Was it because we were young and female and didn't know how to fight back?

Wait.

I went back, held the Doge's image in my mind: the iron-grey hair, the white hands. My fingers probed my cheekbone. He'd been wearing one ring on his right hand. A gold talisman. A gorgon's head.

I opened my eyes.

The mirror in my room, the mirrors in the Doge's ballroom, were surmounted with gorgon's heads.

Gonzaga's ring was the key.

I let out a long, slow breath between my lips. Gorgon's heads were good luck charms. People carved them on doors or wore them on rings to ward away evil. I suspected the Glass Doge was old enough to have known Medusa and her sisters personally. But would his mirrors really open to the cheap silver version Gonzaga wore?

Only one way to find out. I went inside and ordered Maria to bring me Mama's jewellery box. She looked at me doubtfully, but obeyed without speaking.

My sisters were downstairs in the piano nobile. Lucia was playing the spinet and singing, and I momentarily wondered if Gonzaga was with them. Not that it mattered; the Doge's ultimatum had somehow brought us into an uneasy alliance. When Maria brought the jewellery box, I sent her out again and sifted through the jewels until I found Mama's gorgon-head ring.

It was too big and bulky, so she never wore it. I slid it onto my forefinger and walked to the mirror on the wall.

I swallowed. If I could have prayed, I would have.

I reached out my hand. The glass kissed my fingertip.

It was not a cold day, and my hands were not warm. But the surface of the mirror fogged over where I touched it. The fog spread. I pushed—and my finger slid through into the chill beyond.

136

I snatched my hand back and the fog dissipated. My heart and head were both light as air.

I knew Gonzaga's secret. And with it, I would save Filippa.

* * *

That evening, I made Filippa wear the ring around her neck on a long chain, keeping the talisman itself tucked out of sight under her stays.

"It's pressing into my bones." She wriggled her shoulders, pouting a little. "What's so special about this old ring, anyway?"

"It'll bring us good luck. I think we're going to need it."

Filippa looked at me incredulously.

I glanced over my shoulder to make sure that Maria was asleep. She slouched in her chair, breathing heavily, and the cup at her elbow was empty. The door to the guest room stood open, but Gonzaga hadn't come upstairs yet, and the mirror was closed.

I beckoned Filippa to the mirror. When I touched the glass, it resisted me. But when I took her hand and pressed it against the surface, the clear glass fogged over—and let her through.

Filippa shrieked and pulled her hand back. Lucia sat up in bed. "Filippa! You went through!"

Filippa clasped her hands to her chest. "The gorgon ring did that?"

"Hush!" I nodded. "It's the key to opening the mirrors. Not just this one, but the mirrors in the palazzo beyond the glass as well. This will..." I swallowed. "This will keep us from being trapped."

It wouldn't rescue Benito, Pollonia, or anyone else. But maybe, just maybe, it would be enough for us.

"Trapped?" As always, Lucia sensed my fear. "Is something wrong, Gemma? Who would trap us?"

I didn't answer. I happened to be looking into the mirror, and in the reflection I saw Maria slumped in the shadows beyond the bed. There was no sound, but her hand was a pale glimmer as it went up and sketched the sign of the cross.

The hair prickled on my scalp.

Maria was awake.

"Gemma?" Lucia repeated, more softly.

"Yes," I managed. "Yes, something's wrong." I turned and circled the foot of the bed, a heady mix of fear and anger thrumming in my blood. Maria held still, but her breath caught as I approached her.

Without preamble, I pounced on her, catching her by the ear and yanking her out of the chair. "On your knees, you wretch!"

Lucia gasped. Maria's eyes flew open with a muffled shriek of pain, but then she obeyed me, falling prostrate. "Forgive me, signorina! I'm sorry, I'm sorry!"

She was almost hysterical. "Keep your voice down!" I hissed. "Why are you spying on us? Where's the wine?"

138

"I poured it out, signorina! The signor said I must! Please, please, don't accuse me to your mother!"

"The signor?" I grabbed her by the scruff of the neck. "Get up and look me in the eye! Which signor?"

She rose to her knees, her face shiny with tears. "Signor Gonzaga, signorina!"

Gonzaga! I should have known he'd double-cross me. I should have known he'd suborn Maria. I let go of her and stalked across the room.

I'd kept the laudanum pills in my jewellery-box, and when I opened the lid they were gone. He'd even had her remove my supplies. I was surprised when my voice was steady. "And why did he want you awake tonight, Maria?"

"He said that he and I must follow you!"

My sisters watched us with huge eyes. Filippa gasped. "He wants another witness. He's going to tell Papa about us in the morning!"

I shook my head. "No. No, that's not it." I threw open the lid of a linen chest and dug to the bottom of the folded layers. At the very bottom was a small pill-box containing two more laudanum pills—just in case something happened to the others. I took out one of them and advanced on Maria.

There were still tears on her face as I bent over her. "You're going to swallow this, Maria. And you're going to forget anything you might have heard. Do you think Gonzaga means you any good? The lord beyond the glass demands sacrifices, and Gonzaga means to make a

139

sacrifice of *you*."

Lucia clapped a hand over her mouth. *Plague!* I'd forgotten she didn't know about the Doge's bargains. I was slipping.

Maria sniffled. "He said I'd be freed."

"He can't promise you *anything*. You're not his slave." I forced the laudanum pill into her hand. "Be reasonable, Maria. If you obey me, you will sleep all night and everything will be all right in the morning. But if you obey Gonzaga, he'll hand you over to a new and much worse master. Trust me, you're better off here than you are beyond the glass."

I don't know whether it was my logic that convinced her or her own fears. Slowly, she put the pill in her mouth and swallowed. I made her open her mouth afterwards to demonstrate that it was gone. Whole, instead of ground up in wine, the drug took longer to put her to sleep. But she was genuinely unconscious by the time Gonzaga entered the guest-room.

My sisters kept silent as we waited for the mirror to open. I wished I could hear their thoughts. What were they thinking? What did they suspect? Did they still believe in me?

Trading Maria in Filippa's place was obviously Gonzaga's plan. I was glad I'd put a stop to it, but it took away the sense of reassurance I'd had all day. Gonzaga was evidently still willing to double-cross me, had probably been calculating, in that cool brain of his, even as he

140

patted my back and dried my tears. And now I had no safety-net, no second plan to fall back on. It was my own plan or nothing.

That just means I can't fail.

We were already dressed when the mirror opened. For the first time in weeks, I was actually eager to go. I double-checked that Filippa still had the gorgon-ring before we stepped through.

As we made our way down the stairs of the mirror palazzo, I pictured Gonzaga upstairs trying to wake Maria. How dare he promise her her freedom? How dare she betray me like this?

Did she want freedom so badly?

She was only a Tartar. She'd never been born to govern and command either herself or others. Not like me. But did she dream of it like I did?

A clatter of footsteps sounded on the stairs above us. Startled, I nearly dropped the candle, but when we turned to look upstairs it was only Gonzaga. He nodded to Filippa and Lucia, and offered his arm to me. "May I?"

I let my fingers rest on his sleeve. He bent his head to my ear, his whisper taut and angry. "What reason, Gemma? I thought you wanted my help!"

Safest to play the fool. I widened innocent eyes at him.

As we reached the foot of the stairs, he pulled me aside, waving Filippa and Lucia ahead of us. "I would have traded Maria for your sister," he hissed.

"I don't see why you should presume to do that. Maria

141

is Caloprini property."

"She would have been by far the simplest option!" For the first time since I'd known him, Gonzaga seemed genuinely upset, and I didn't know why. But he didn't stop to explain. Instead, he dropped my hand and wheeled around to join my sisters. I followed them to the door and signalled for the gondolas. Wondering.

Across the canal, up the stairs, into the Doge's ballroom. Great mirrors made of perfect glass without a flaw lined the walls. Stealthily, I pressed my fingers against the nearest. Cold, smooth glass. I had to trust that they would open for Filippa.

"Do you see the Doge?" Gonzaga spoke in my ear, making me jump.

I scanned the room. No sign of the Doge, and it was necessary that I should find him before Gonzaga did. "No, I don't."

Gonzaga gave a perfunctory bow and left me. I waited until he was out of earshot, then spoke in a conversational tone: "Your serenity, a word?"

From the people near me, I received startled glances, and more than one person hurriedly moved away. But a short woman in a mask turned to look up, and I recognised the vacant eyes of one who had become little more than a puppet for the Doge.

"Have you brought me a life, Gemma Caloprini?"

I lowered my voice. "I will. Tonight. But I wanted to warn you about Gonzaga. He thinks it's Lucia who hasn't

142

been paid for yet. Don't tell him it's really Filippa."

"Why not?"

Because then he'll know I'm lying to him, and he needs to trust me if I'm going to save my sister. I didn't tell the Doge this. "Because I want his help paying my debts, and the only way to get it is if he thinks it's Lucia who's in danger."

He'll bring you lives, I wanted to add. But I couldn't let the Doge see how desperate I was.

"I see." He paused, or he let his puppet of flesh pause. "It makes no difference to me. One way or another, I get paid."

The Doge's puppet staggered back suddenly with a whimper of pain. He'd left her, and he'd made me no promises. Once more, I scanned the room for him, but he was still nowhere to be seen.

Perhaps it was just as well. If he knew how much this meant to me, he'd use the knowledge against me. Even if he gave his word, I knew by now that he would keep it only as long as it suited him.

Maybe I should have let Gonzaga sacrifice Maria after all.

Someone asked me to dance. As we took our places in the set, one of the mirrors rippled and Gonzaga emerged looking thoughtful. The Doge followed on his heels. So they had gone aside to talk!

Gonzaga caught me staring, and one eyelid dropped in a wink.

I turned my head quickly. Despite the wink, I could

143

tell he was crestfallen, his face sombre. That calmed my apprehensions. Anything that bothered Gonzaga could only be good news for me. I would stick to my plan.

One way or another, my sister was coming home tonight.

* * *

Night was fading into day when I sought out Gonzaga.

I'd left it as long as I dared. Now it was finally time to act, my heart seemed to be trying to crawl up my throat for fear that I'd left it too late, that the sunrise would catch us all beyond the glass.

I pushed my way through the crowd and put my hand on his arm. "A word?"

The loggia was cool and dark with the chilly dawn breezes running through it. When Gonzaga and I arrived, a knot of laughing people abruptly got up and filed out.

Clearly the Doge meant us to have all the privacy we wanted.

"What have you arranged with him?" I whispered.

He tilted an eyebrow.

"Don't do that. I know you spoke with him. I saw you come through the glass."

He gave half a smile. "I found something to trade for your sister's freedom."

"What is it? Tell me."

A brittle laugh. "After everything else, you'll forgive me

144

if I don't trust you with that information."

Some of my confidence evaporated. "So it's something I won't like."

"Maybe so. But your sister will be safe. That's what you want, isn't it? More than anything else?"

It was. But I was too wary of him to admit it.

"Gemma…" He'd taken my silence as a negative. "Nothing comes without a price. There's always got to be a sacrifice. The only question is whether you make it yourself or get someone else to make it for you."

I looked at him with contempt. Hypocrite, speaking of sacrifice and doing his best to avoid paying the required price himself. "People ought to make their own sacrifices and stop exploiting other people."

"I'm glad you take that view." His voice was weary. Sombre.

I didn't know what to do with his agreement. I'd expected a fight, but at least he seemed sincere, no longer on his guard. After a moment I put out my hand. "I'm grateful for your help, signor. Really."

He stirred himself and smiled, taking my hand. "Call me Cosimo. After all, we're to be kin."

"Cosimo." I tasted the name warily.

His hand firmed. "I never said I was sorry."

I'd been staring at the gorgon ring on the hand that held mine. At his words, I jerked my head up, wondering if I'd heard correctly. "Sorry? For what?"

"For nearly getting you killed that night in the alley."

145

His eyes were shadowed. "For everything. I wish..."

He didn't finish his sentence. I didn't breathe. He was apologising. To me. I finally found a name for that strange emotion in his eyes. Regret.

He shook it off and smirked. "Now's your chance to admit it, Gemma. I'm not as bad as you thought."

All I could think was that I was about to betray him. That I would in some sense be his murderer. It was as if he'd whisked the floor out from under my feet—or if not the floor, then my excuse for what I was about to do.

Could I go through with this plan?

For Filippa. I had to save her. *For Lucia.* She deserved better than Gonzaga.

Now I was the one looking sombre. I swallowed, forced a smile. "I've never had a brother before."

He was laughing. "Then you're about to start enjoying yourself."

I still held his hand; my fingertips brushed the gorgon ring. As casually as I could, I glanced down and said, "Is that the ring you won at dice? May I see it?"

I waited for him to narrow his eyes. To mock me for thinking he could be such a fool. But he didn't. He let me draw him to the rail of the loggia where the light was stronger.

"Women and their trinkets," he said with a laugh.

My heartbeat kicked up in tempo. I'd teach him to underestimate me. The ring sat lightly on his littlest finger; I whisked it off before he realised what I was doing.

146

And then with a flick of my wrist I threw it out, out, out…

It faded into the grey morning light. And in the sighing of the dawn wind, I did not even hear its splash as the canal swallowed it.

"Plague it, Gemma," Gonzaga began, perplexed. And then, more sharply: "What have you done?"

He reached for me, but I tripped back a few steps, unsure whether to laugh or cry. "Your talisman. Your way out." Laughter it was, then. "Best go diving for it, signor. You'll need it."

"Plague!" Reflexively, he clasped his hands together, only now realising what he'd lost.

I didn't dare to wait. My plan had worked, and it was time to leave him to his fate. I flicked around and ran for the ballroom.

A hand fastened mercilessly on my wrist.

"Not so fast," Gonzaga snarled.

I had the door open. I could see Filippa and Lucia waiting next to the closest mirror, right where I'd warned them to be. Ten steps, and if we made it through the mirror ahead of Gonzaga, he would be trapped and our debt would be paid.

I could almost smell the freedom.

I threw all my weight against him, but he was much stronger than I expected.

"Hold still!" He captured my other wrist. *"You're* my talisman now!"

"Let go! Let go, you're hurting me!"

147

Our scuffle attracted attention within the room. The music faltered, and the crowd thickened toward us, blocking my sisters from sight. *Plague!*

"Not a hope. I've underestimated you once too often." Gonzaga shook his head with a short laugh. "*Diabolo!* How I wish I'd had you with me in Milan. You're wasted in Venice."

"Let *go* of me!" Each moment we wasted here, the sun came closer to rising. My panic mounted. "Doge! Help!"

"Ah, yes, the Doge! Let's find him, shall we?"

I'd been pulling against Gonzaga, but now he shifted his weight, and we staggered into the crowded ballroom, scattering the onlookers. For a moment amidst the shifting bodies I saw Filippa. She had the gorgon ring ready: the silver chain around her neck snaked into her white-knuckled fist and disappeared. "Gemma," she pleaded, but I only saw her pale lips move. Another moment, I realised, and her fear would drive her through the mirrors, abandoning me to my fate. I lunged to free myself of Gonzaga's grip, but he held to me as grimly as death. "Wait for me!" I shrieked at her.

"Doge!" Gonzaga shouted, dragging me further into the room.

The bodies parted, and the tall black figure came toward us.

I opened my mouth to say that I had stolen Gonzaga's talisman and my payment could now be made. But Gonzaga spoke first, and his words took the breath from my lungs.

"Here's your payment, Doge. As promised."

He shoved and released my wrists in the same movement. Caught on the wrong foot, I crumbled to the floor at the Doge's feet.

Payment. He'd told me he found something to trade for my sister's freedom.

Me.

I turned, looking up at him in utter shock.

He returned a twisted smile. The regret was back in his eyes. "You said people ought to make their own sacrifices, Gemma. Here's your chance."

The crowd surged, and Lucia burst through with wild eyes. With squeaking protests, Filippa followed in her tracks, still clutching the ring. But Lucia paid no heed to her. "Gemma!"

Gonzaga held my gaze a moment. "I didn't want to do it. I tried." Then he grabbed Lucia around the waist and steered her toward the mirrors, scattering onlookers right and left. Evidently, he still didn't believe the ring was a talisman.

I clambered to my feet and turned to the Doge. "I'm trying to *pay* you!"

He smiled thinly. "One way or another, my dear."

Useless. I wheeled to follow the condottiere.

He reached the mirrors, thudded into glass, and reeled back again with a curse. Lucia took her opportunity and twisted out of his grip. Then I reached them, latched onto

Gonzaga's arm, and held on like death.

"Let go," he growled, trying to shake me off. "Is this *your* doing?" He jerked his head at the mirrors. "Did you do this?"

Of course I had, I'd told him so, but he wasn't thinking straight. I had to get him away from Lucia and the mirrors long enough to let the rest of us escape. "Doge! Someone! Hold him!" I begged, but no one lifted a finger.

Filippa dragged Lucia away from us. "Gemma, please! Let go of him! The sun's rising!"

"No!" I shrieked, but she reached out, and her hand broke the surface of a mirror.

Gonzaga stiffened with new shock. "Is that it," he grated. "You have a ring as well!"

Plague! I got a hand behind me and grabbed his belt just as he tried to spin me around and shove me back into the room. I planted my feet and yanked him after me, and then we were in each other's arms, something the deadly opposite of an embrace, each fighting to hold back the other and yet, somehow, to flee to where my sisters stood by the open mirror.

"Children, children!" The Doge advanced to meet us.

Gonzaga and I stilled, still grasping handfuls of each others' clothes and hair. I had no breath left at all, but Gonzaga said, "Doge, you promised…"

"Yes." He looked greatly amused. "As did you promise. Both of you. Each has vowed me the other." He spread his hands in a shrug. "And here you are checkmated,

150

with sunrise no further away than would serve to say a paternoster. It seems both of you must stay."

In the silence that followed, Filippa called my name again, her voice nearly hysterical. "Gemma! *Please!*"

"Leave us." Gonzaga turned to her. "Go! Save yourselves!"

Leave us. Leave us to the Doge. Trapped here forever, never to leave, never to own myself again. Alone...

I screamed: "No! Don't leave! Stay with me!"

I do not think I will ever forget the sound of the silence, the agony on Filippa's face, or the moment of unguarded shock in Gonzaga's eyes that told me, even now, that he'd thought better of me than this...

He turned back to my sisters. "What are you waiting for? Go!"

With a sob, Filippa pulled Lucia toward the mirror. But Lucia cried "No!" and twisted from her grip.

Filippa lifted despairing hands.

Lucia was pallidly resolute, her eyes enormous. She came toward us with her fair hair ruffled and standing out from her head in a halo; I was terrifyingly reminded of how she had looked when she gave our shoes to Papa and began all the trouble.

"Only one person needs to stay," she said to Gonzaga.

"No," he shouted. "No, Lucia."

She circled him and faced the Doge. Amazingly, he retreated a step. "I have given you no leave to speak!" he said.

She paid no heed to any of it. "Take me instead, your serenity. Tell them they can leave."

* * *

All this was happening, and I was aware of it; painfully aware, as a mortal can be only once or twice in a lifetime. But at the same time—and the time seemed to hover and wait for me—it was as if I saw myself as well, the way I had seen myself mirrored in Filippa's horrified eyes as I screamed for her to stay and share my prison.

I am not selfish. I would share it with the whole city, if I could.

Was this what I had become?

Had I been looking into mirrors so long and never truly seen myself? Lucia was doing what I ought to have done. But it had never crossed my mind.

I, with my talk of sacrifice.

I let go of Gonzaga and blurted, "No, Lucia! You go. I'll stay."

* * *

Too little, too late. No one heard me. All eyes were on my sister. The Doge backed another step. A faint sighing and rustling went through the room, and when I turned, I saw that everyone in it had gone blank-eyed; they shuffled forward under the Doge's compulsion.

Arms reached and clung to me; a hand sought my mouth, as if to stifle any words I might say. By the mirrors, Filippa screamed; Gonzaga gave a yell of panic and fumbled for his rapier; I saw Benito, nightmarishly vacant, grab for Lucia.

She stretched out a hand to the Doge. "Come back! I'll be your sacrifice, if you'll have me."

She may yet save us, Papa had said.

I didn't know what was happening. But I could see the Doge's fear. I knew he preferred his sacrifices helpless and terrified. What would happen if someone sacrificed herself willingly? Not because they had been tricked or forced, but out of love?

I fought the clinging hands away from my face. "Your name! Give him your name!"

She heard me this time. "I am Lucia Caloprini, and I give my life for theirs."

I know that what I have to say seems impossible to believe, even to myself who was there. But the reader has followed me this far. Let him show charity a little longer, and I will say truthfully what I saw.

The Doge threw his head back and howled.

The skin on his face cracked and peeled away like paper in the scorching heat of a fire, like a mask thrown into the flames. A strong hot wind slammed through the loggia windows and swept through the room toward him. Curtains and dresses billowed, and I lost sight of the Doge, but his howls no longer seemed to come from mortal lungs. They seemed part of the air itself, so loud that I thought my head would burst.

Then the glass broke.

Each mirror on the wall bloomed into a cloud of jagged, deadly shards. A thousand shattered reflections surged through the air toward me; dimly, I saw Filippa in the midst of them with her head bent and her arms up in a useless attempt to protect herself. I gave a wail of despair as they cut through me like cold knives.

The next thing I remember is opening my eyes.

I was so peaceful, so painless, so calm that for a moment I thought I was dead. Then sensation returned to me. The first thing I noticed was bone-numbing cold, as if I'd just traversed a mirror. The second was that my legs were pinned under a dead weight and wouldn't move. The third was the diffused grey light of a foggy dawn in late winter.

I peeled myself off the dusty wood of an old floor. Huddled bodies lay on the boards around me and one had fallen across my legs. We lay in a cold, echoing room in the piano nobile of a derelict palazzo. The walls were lined with the ancient frames of mirrors, but all the glass was broken out of them.

The weight on my legs lifted. Gonzaga rolled over and sat up with a groan.

"Gemma."

Lucia's voice was a creaky whisper. She sat in the centre of the room with her knees drawn up to her chest. Beyond

154

her, Filippa was still upright, clinging to one of the mirror-frames, one hand still clenched on the useless gorgon ring.

"Gemma," Lucia whispered again.

Benito knelt on the bare floorboards in front of her. His arms hung bonelessly by his sides, and when he turned his head to speak to me, his eyes were empty.

"Do you think you can steal away like this, signorina? Do you think you'll escape my vengeance?"

I swallowed what felt like a dry lump in my throat. But I was done with the Doge. "What vengeance could you possibly wreak on me? Your house is fallen. And while it stood, you could not even lay a hand on us to keep us within it against our will. I was a fool not to see that sooner."

"You will go to a convent," Benito spat. "When your father hears what you have done he will be so afraid that he will lock you far, far away from the sun. You will never see your sisters again." He turned his head again. "And you, Signor Gonzaga. Have you forgotten that you offered me triple the number of lives if I released Friuli and Mafei? Now you will spend the rest of your days wondering what else I could have done for you, if you had only had the courage to ask."

Gonzaga made no reply. And the Doge had no more chance to speak. Without another word, Benito crumpled to the ground like a suit of cast-off clothes.

A warm tinge of diffused gold crept through the windows. The sun had risen. All over the room, the

155

sleepers began to shift and to sigh and to sit up.

"Benito!" Lucia fell to her knees by his side and shook him. "Benito, wake up!"

I held my breath, knowing that if he did not wake up, if he was gone forever, that it was my doing. That I had killed him.

But he gave a groan and stirred. I dared to look. Benito blinked into my sister's face.

"Lucia?" he whispered. Then he buried his face in her shoulder, his back heaving with sobs. "Lucia! Oh ciel, the dreams I've had!"

* * *

By ones and twos the Doge's guests slunk from the ancient palazzo, picking their way through side doors into the narrow alleys behind the building. Masked in their dancing finery, anyone might mistake them for late revellers hastening back to their homes.

If they still had homes. If not, the hospitals and convents of the city were going to be filled with supplicants.

One of them came to me hesitantly before she left. I recognised Pollonia by her dress and mask, and stepped aside to speak to her.

"I came to say thanks," she whispered shyly.

I swallowed. "It wasn't I who freed you. Lucia did that."

"I know." Pollonia couldn't repress a chuckle and nodded to where Lucia was still sitting on the floor, holding Benito's hand. "She was the only one who figured it out. I tried to tell you, so often, but I never could."

I dropped my gaze. "If I'd known it was so simple…"

"Then it would have been no true sacrifice." She spoke gently, but the words were condemning. "Thank her for me, when she's ready."

She turned.

"Wait! Where are you going?"

Pollonia looked back, and I sensed her uncertainty. "To walk to and fro in the Daylight City."

I didn't know how much I would be able to help her, even if Papa would let me. Still, after what she had just said, it seemed impossible not to offer. "If you need help, Pollonia…come to the Caloprini palazzo."

I'd never told anyone here my name. Now, after a short silence, Pollonia reached up and took off her mask. I'd never seen the face beneath. It was a little older, a little plainer, a little more tired than I expected.

She smiled sadly. "I will. Thank you."

There was no reason to stay. Benito was still wobbly on his feet, but Lucia was able to hold him steady. Gonzaga found Signor Friuli in a corner, and almost had to carry the old man. He seemed to be looking into an endless gulf that only he could see; his eyes haunted me.

We made our way downstairs into the damp vestibule of the abandoned palazzo. Gonzaga set Friuli on the floor while he went out to hail a gondola. Benito protested to Lucia that he could stand on his own feet. But Filippa grabbed my arm and pulled me aside with a grip like a drowning man's.

"Gemma," she whispered roughly, "did you know? About what the Doge did to them? The blank eyes, the—the control?"

I closed my eyes in shame. There was hardly any sound in the word: "Yes."

There was a silence. I braced myself for her indignation.

"I ought to have known," she said raggedly.

That shocked my eyes open. "I was the one who deceived you."

She took no notice of that. "I *did* know. I knew, and I winked at it! Oh, Gemma, I'm sorry."

I didn't know why she was apologising to me, but at that moment Gonzaga came back in to say that he had found a gondola with room in it for all six of us. We followed him out the door and into the Daylight City.

Slowly, the burdened craft lumbered across the Great Canal. The city was well awake by now: alive with merchants and senators, canal brats and beggars, travellers and craftsmen. Most of them had somewhere to be, something to do. This banker would spend his day sitting on the Rialto bridge, entering numbers in a ledger for his passing customers. That gondolier slid smartly through the water to collect a passenger. That errand-boy puffed his way down the fondamenta with a message wrinkled between his fingers.

Once, I'd have envied them their freedom. Now, in the wide morning, with sunshine reflecting from the surface of the water and welling up into a haze shot with blue shadow and yellow light, I saw them differently. They were all servants to somebody, even if only to the passersby who engaged their services for an hour.

Perhaps what set them apart from me was not so much their freedom as their purpose. All this time, trapped in the convent or my father's house, I could have found some form of exchange similar to theirs. I could have had something to do, perhaps even somewhere to go. I might not have been given my freedom, Papa might even have fought to keep me from earning it…but there was more for me here in the Daylight City than I'd ever tried to find.

And instead, I had run away beyond the glass, and nearly been trapped there forever.

If I was given a second chance, I vowed, I would act differently.

The gondola bumped against our front doorstep. Gonzaga paid the fare and one by one we clambered out and ventured in the front door. There were running footsteps upstairs, and confused voices. Then Maria leaned over the banister above and stared at us, speechless.

Papa followed Maria, saw us, and erupted into puzzled words. Where had we been? Why did we leave the house? Was that really Benito and Friuli? He took the stairs two at a time and then stood still at the foot of them, staring at us all as if a miracle had occurred, waiting for us to answer.

Nobody, it seemed, was willing to speak. It was Lucia who broke the silence.

"We're home now, Papa."

* * *

It all had to come out. Friuli was left downstairs wrapped in a rug with a heated posset to calm him while the rest of us squeezed into Papa's study.

"This is a miracle, Cosimo," Papa said, rubbing his hands. "A miracle. You cannot conceive how this sets my mind at rest."

Gonzaga didn't answer right away. From the back of the room, Filippa said in a small voice, "He went upstairs. I don't know why."

There was a moment's silence.

"It's all right," I said wearily. "I'll tell you what's been happening, Papa."

His eyebrows climbed. *"Gemma?"*

There were excuses I could have made for my silence, good ones. But they could come later. I began to tell the story, but Papa interrupted almost at once.

"A city beyond the mirrors? What kind of tale is this?"

"It's true," Benito protested weakly from behind me, but Papa didn't hear him. Instead, he got to his feet with the tip of his nose turning white.

"This is too much, Gemma! You have done nothing but defy me, and now you think you can cozen me with an untruth?"

"It's true," Gonzaga called from the door.

We all turned. He didn't look me in the eye; he hadn't since the glass broke. He shouldered his way past Lucia and Filippa, past Benito and me, and laid three items down on the desk in front of Papa. The first was a silver goblet, the second was the golden candlestick I'd glimpsed the previous morning, and the third was a lady's necklace shimmering with precious stones, which I was sure I'd seen on Pollonia.

"I brought them back from the glass city." Gonzaga cleared his throat. "They—looked like they might be worth something."

Silently, Papa picked up the necklace, weighing it in his hand as if he was weighing our story.

"It's only glass," Gonzaga added. "Worthless. Couldn't get a ducat for the lot of them."

Papa looked up. "You're telling me this story is *true?*"

This time, Benito made himself heard. "Every word."

Papa turned back to Gonzaga. "You mean to tell me that you've known about this for days? Why didn't you tell me?"

Gonzaga hitched a shoulder. "What point in merely telling you about the glass? What useful action could you have taken? I promised you I'd free Mafei and Friuli before asking for a bride."

Papa looked from Gonzaga to Benito, then to my sisters, before finally returning to me with a strange new note of respect in his voice. "I'm sorry, Gemma. Go on."

It wasn't an easy story to tell, and I had taken my mask off to tell it properly. The room was silent as I spoke. I had kept so many secrets for so long that everyone was hearing something new, even my sisters.

When I finished, Papa stared at the false treasures on his desk, tugging his beard.

My heart dropped when he spoke. "I suppose that means you have won the hand of my youngest daughter, Cosimo."

"Papa," Lucia protested.

I'd told the story as honestly as I could with regards to Gonzaga. We had both been self-serving and treacherous, but it was impossible to hide how much I'd done to save Lucia from him. Papa should understand her feelings by now.

Still, he remained inexorable. "I promised, Lucia."

She looked down, and after a moment, she stole her hand away from Benito. I swallowed. This too was my fault.

Beside me, Gonzaga shifted uneasily. "Perhaps not all promises should be kept, signor."

There was an expression on his face that I had never seen there before. Shame.

"Signorina Lucia is too good for me." He seemed to be speaking to the papers on the desk, not to Papa himself.

162

"I'm too much of a rascal for a child like her. Besides, it's Signorina Gemma who has met the conditions of the wager and told you where your daughters spend their time. Since she cannot marry Lucia, perhaps you should allow *her* to choose her sister's husband."

Papa's mouth actually dropped open. I stared at Gonzaga in disbelief, but he still didn't meet my gaze.

"She's earned it," he added.

Papa closed his mouth and swung around to inspect me as if I was some fantastic creature from the Antipodes. It took him a moment to get the words out.

"Gemma? Who—what do *you* think?"

I opened my mouth, but caught myself just in time and closed it again. Lucia was looking at me trustfully. I didn't know why, not after everything I'd done. For a moment some of my old exasperation came back. Would she never stop fawning on the hands that beat her?

Yet she'd saved all of us. From the mess that *my* efforts had gotten us into.

I shook my head. "You should ask Lucia, Papa. She's the one who saved us. Including Benito and Signor Friuli. And she's the one who will have to marry."

Dazed, Papa turned to Lucia.

For a wonder, she wasn't slow to speak. She blushed wildly and stammered. "I don't know, Papa. W-we could get to know Benito a little better?"

Her hand stole into his once again as the two of them looked hopeful. Papa blinked and looked at Gonzaga, and then at me, and then at Lucia, as if trying to trace the exact progression by which he'd ended up asking his youngest daughter for her opinion on her marriage.

"Maybe we could," he conceded.

Finally, Gonzaga managed to look at me. And winked.

* * *

This morning, the mirror in our bedroom was nothing more than a candid sheet of glass. All the same, my heartbeat sped up as I slipped Mama's gorgon ring onto my forefinger. It took a moment to work up my courage. Then I touched the cold surface.

I counted to ten. When I took my finger away, there was only an oval fingerprint on the clear glass.

Maria's voice broke into my thoughts. "Signor Gonzaga is leaving, signorina."

Leaving. Despite everything, the word hit me like a clenched fist. I didn't want Gonzaga to leave. Not after—everything.

My eyes didn't leave the fingerprint on the glass. "I'll come down," I managed.

But to my surprise, booted feet echoed on the marble floor, and I looked up to see his reflection coming toward me.

I turned, folding my hands.

His eyebrow flickered as he glanced from the gorgon ring to the mirror-frame behind. "What's this, Gemma?

Already tired of the Daylight?"

My cheeks burned. "No such thing! I only wanted to know if I had to smash it." I half-turned and laid my hand against the glass once more. "See? The magic is gone. I think I'll keep it."

"It's a good clear glass."

"The better to see my faults in."

He snorted. "You're still too young to have many faults, Gemma."

"Not like you—is that what you mean?"

The corners of his mouth twisted with savage humour. "I won't tell you I'm sorry. I am, but you wouldn't believe me."

For a moment he looked into my eyes.

"In that case, maybe I'll try believing." Before he could say anything, I changed the subject. "What are you going to do now, signor? Isn't there still a price on your head?"

He looked away. "Seems like it."

"What are you going to do about it?"

"I'll run. Maybe to Rhodes. I hear there's trouble brewing with the Turks; ought to be good employment for a man of my talents, and a chance to earn what I need to pay Sforza."

A silence.

"What about you? Will your father send you to a convent?"

"We haven't talked about it."

The gold network of reflections danced on the ceiling.

"Although," I added, "maybe I can find a way to change his mind. Offer him something he wants."

Gonzaga grinned at me. Then he tilted his head, scratching his jaw. "Let's see, what does Caloprini want?"

I spoke on impulse. "A son-in-law."

"Benito, though…" He lifted his eyebrows.

I shook my head. "Benito's an only son and a skilled glassblower. Whether he marries Lucia or not, he'll have to take over his father's workshop. Papa wants someone who doesn't already have a calling, someone to learn the business and carry it on when he dies." I couldn't repress a smile. "Someone with a good head for making deals."

He grinned. "You almost tempt me to try for a new Caloprini alliance."

I smiled as impudently as I knew how. "Do I? I'm so glad you understand me."

Slowly, the smile faded from his lips, and he dropped his gaze.

I tried to keep my voice light. "You need not worry about corrupting *my* innocence."

He looked up again, the cynical twist back in his mouth. "I called you a hellcat, didn't I? My dear, I don't know if you're quite hellcat enough to deserve me."

"And if not you, then who?" My voice wavered on the edge of all my fears. "My reputation is in tatters—thanks to you. And who would I take, anyway? I'm too much the hellcat for the likes of Benito."

"Gemma!" His voice sharpened. "Don't you know me

166

by now, girl? Thirty years I've been a braggart and a freebooter; do you really think I'll change now?"

"Is this about the money?" I flung back at him. "Because—"

"*Yes*, it's about the damned money!" His raised voice sent echoes skittering through the room. He shot Maria a sideways glance and stepped closer, lowering his voice. "I would have sold your soul for the sake of that money. If I took it now, would I deserve you? Would I be the kind of man who could make you happy?"

I'd never dreamed of there being anything so tender as *love* between us. But in that moment, I could imagine it.

"No," I said, "you wouldn't."

He huffed in a breath. Then out again. Then he stood back, straightening, rolling his shoulders, reaching for my hand. "Where there's a patrimony there's a paramour, Gemma." He bent to kiss my hand. "Never fails."

"So you'll come back."

He stiffened.

"You'll pay your debt, and you'll come back." I was sure of myself now. "And we can talk about it again."

He stared at me for a moment as if I'd sprouted a second head. And then, with a roll of the eyes and a chuckle, he surrendered.

"Not if the Turks get me first."

"If they do, then you are no man for me."

He had a nice smile when he really meant it. "It's a deal," he said.

As Maria turned to follow him from the room, I said, "Maria? Don't go."

I didn't have a chance to say anything else, because at that moment the door to the guest-room burst open and my sisters rustled through it. "Gemma! Did he ask for your hand?"

I stared at them.

"Papa was keen on it." Filippa lifted an eyebrow, scanning my face for a reaction. "We heard them talking about it."

Well.

I tipped up my nose. "He's a braggart and a freebooter. What do you *think* I said?"

Through the sound of their groans, from Mama's room next door, we heard the bell ring. Maria shifted. "Signorina, I'm wanted."

"One moment!" I darted for the dressing-table. The purse I'd offered Gonzaga yesterday afternoon was still lying there: my few valuable jewels and all the money I had. It wasn't much to a man like Gonzaga. But to Maria, it might mean everything.

I snatched it up and held it out to her. "Here. This is for you."

Maria was puzzled. "Do you wish me to take it somewhere, signorina?"

"That's right." My heart was lighter than I'd ever felt it before. "Or why don't we go together? Let's take it to Mama and buy your freedom."

S.D.G.

Historical Note

There are some wonderful things in the history of Venice. The city began as a small settlement of refugees on the islands of the Veneto lagoon. The water provided safety from invaders during the early Middle Ages, but it also limited the amount of land available. In feudal Europe, ambitious lords competed for land and the result was regular small-scale warfare. But in Venice, land wasn't the basis of the economy, trade was. And with trade booming throughout the Mediterranean, ambitious Venetians didn't have to fight each other in order to get rich. Venetian politics was similarly characterised by peace and stability. The result was a republic that became a major world power and lasted a staggering thousand years, gaining its influence and glory primarily through service, not force.

But there is also a dark side to Venetian history. Some examples crop up in this story, including the famous Murano glassmakers who were forbidden to leave the lagoon for fear of compromising the Venetian monopoly on fine glass. Slavery was always a brisk business in the medieval Mediterranean, but the trade in Tartar, Turkish,

Greek, Russian, and other slaves boomed during the early Renaissance after the arrival of bubonic plague in 1348 wiped out much of the working class and caused serious manpower shortages. But the Venetian patricians didn't stop at oppressing commoners and strangers: they treated their children almost as badly. For various complex dynastic reasons, only one son and one daughter in each generation was usually permitted to marry during this period. The remaining sons resorted to the famous Venetian courtesans to find the companionship which was denied them in marriage, while the spare daughters were locked into convents. At the height of this practice late in the sixteenth century, nearly sixty percent of all patrician women in Venice lived in convents, and the majority of them were there against their will. While married women were able to leverage their family ties and massive dowries to attain a measure of economic freedom, most were never so fortunate. Meanwhile, as I have Gonzaga point out, even sons did not attain legal majority until their fathers either died or emancipated them.

As a keen amateur historian, I'm accustomed to wincing when people assume that all women living before about 1920 were ignorant, oppressed, and unable to inherit or control property (as if world history was not long and diverse and filled with creative, bold, and influential women). Venetian history surprised me because, for a limited time during the Renaissance, it actually *was* that bad. Thankfully, the practice of forcing the majority of young women into convents (or monachisation) was unsustainably wasteful and had to be abandoned within a few generations. But the patricians of Venice would struggle to repair the demographic disaster and many old and proud families became extinct.

Those familiar with Venetian history will notice at least one major anachronism. The monachisations reached their height in the century between 1550 and 1650. On the other hand, after the 1453 fall of Constantinople to the Ottoman Turks, Venetian involvement in the slave trade was choked off as the Ottomans closed the ports of the Black Sea and Eastern Mediterranean to Christian merchants, thus shifting the slave trade (infamously) to the Atlantic. So, in reality, the slave trade was *not* contemporaneous with the forced monachisations. But I found both things too fascinating not to include in the same story.

I'd like to acknowledge some of my sources: Thomas F. Madden's book *Venice: A New History* was a readable introduction to the story of this unique city. Jutta Gisela Sperling's book *Convents and the Body Politic in Late Renaissance Venice*—or at any rate the part of it I was able to read on Google Books—was a fascinating study of how and why so many patrician women were imprisoned in convents. And Iris Origo's classic article "The Domestic Enemy: The Eastern Slaves in Tuscany in the Fourteenth and Fifteen Centuries" (*Speculum*, Vol. 30, No. 3 [Jul.,

1955], pp. 321-366) provided helpful information on Italian Renaissance involvement in the slave trade.

Suzannah Rowntree

February 2018

About the Author

Suzannah Rowntree lives in a big house in rural Australia with her awesome parents and siblings, reading academic histories of the Crusades and writing historical fantasy fiction that blends folklore and myth with historical fact. She is the author of the historical fantasy series *Watchers of Outremer* as well as the Arthurian fantasy *Pendragon's Heir* and a series of fairytale retellings.

You can connect with me on:

🌐 https://suzannahrowntree.site

🐦 https://twitter.com/suzannahtweets

Subscribe to my newsletter:

✉ https://www.subscribepage.com/srauthor

Also by Suzannah Rowntree

The Fairy Tale Retold Series
The Rakshasa's Bride
The Prince of Fishes
The Bells of Paradise
Death Be Not Proud
Ten Thousand Thorns
The City Beyond the Glass

The Pendragon's Heir Trilogy
The Door to Camelot
The Quest for Carbonek
The Heir of Logres

The Watchers of Outremer Series
Children of the Desolate
A Wind from the Wilderness
The Lady of Kingdoms